Loving You

Copyright

Fourth Edition, February 2023
Copyright © 2023 by Melony Ann

Paperback ISBN: 978-1-961966-00-0

Published by: Carxander Publishing
Minnesota

Disclaimer

The books in this series are based completely on dreams that I've had or that one of the other people in my relationship has had. They all have a little bit of real life thrown in so that you, the reader, can get to know us a little bit better.

These books can and should be read as standalone books. There isn't an order to them. All of the characters in the books are the same, as they are all based on characters from real life.

As you read these books, please keep in mind that other than the characters and the city they are based in, these books are not connected to other books in the series. They aren't a continuation of other books. They are all novellas based on dreams that revolve around the same characters.

As you keep that in mind, please enjoy reading this book. I do hope you will also read the others in this series and love them as much as I loved writing them!

Opening Quote

Make a promise please, that you'll always be in reach. Just in case I need you there when I call. This is all so new. Seems too good to be true. Could this really be a safe place to fall?

Lightweight by Demi Lovato

Chapter One

☆ Mariah ☆

I can't believe it! Stupid GPS. How is this possible? How does a GPS, something that is supposed to help keep me from getting lost, GET ME LOST?

This is so stupid.

And how the hell is it so hot?

So incredibly hot.

I feel tears stinging my eyes.

No.

I will absolutely not cry.

I won't.

I will figure this out.

I pull over to the side of the road and take several deep breaths. I close my eyes for a moment and clear out my GPS. I put the address for Arbor Park Apartments into the GPS again and let it figure it out.

Once again, tears sting my eyes. I fight them, but one escapes. I reach up and vigorously wipe it away.

No.

I'm not doing this. I cried the entire way down here. I will not allow myself to cry anymore. I've wasted enough tears over him. Both of them. No more.

I glance at my GPS and see it still isn't working. It's all it takes for the dam to break. The tears burst from my eyes, and I put my head down on my steering wheel.

Why would it work for me? Nothing ever works for me. I've probably just made the biggest mistake of my life. Who the fuck just picks up and moves like that? From one hemisphere to another? Away from everything she's ever known and ever loved?

Obviously me. I do that. I'm so stupid. I've just ruined my entire life.

I jump nearly a mile at the light tap on my window. I turn and see the hottest guy I have ever seen in my life, and for a moment, I'm stunned. He's tall. His hair is short and dark brown. His face looks like it's chiseled out of marble with a hint of scruff that makes him look even sexier. His eyes are the color of coffee. I've never liked brown eyes, but I could drown in his.

I glance in my rearview mirror and see a squad car. The guy is wearing a Gainesville Police Department uniform with Sergeant stripes. He's incredibly muscular, but I am not totally sure if it's the uniform and all of his equipment and gear that make him look like that. His left arm is covered in tattoos as well as some of his right.

I quickly compose myself, wiping my tears as I hit the button to roll down my window. He probably thinks I'm drunk. Or crazy. Or maybe both.

"H-hi."

"Hey. I'm Sergeant Chance of Gainesville PD. Uh… are you… okay?" he asks me, his voice laced with concern. I close my eyes and take a deep breath, willing the tears away as I nod and force my eyes to open again. "Can I help you out with something? Anything?"

"I'm so sorry," I say as he glances in the back of my SUV. "I'm just so lost."

"Okay. Well, I've lived here almost my whole life. Where are you trying to go?"

"Um…" I reach over and hand him my folder with my lease and information for my new apartment. His voice is so calm, steady. He opens the folder and looks at it.

"Okay. Arbor Park Apartments. You're in 4-4834. You're not too far away." He hands me back the folder. I take it and set it back on the seat next to me. "How about you just follow me?"

"Oh. Um. That's okay. I don't want to take you away from your job."

"Well, helping people is my job. Right now you need help. So you're my job." He gives me a killer smile, and my insides melt.

I can't help but smile back. "If you're sure…"

"I am." He glances at the traffic. "I'll pull up alongside you with my lights on. Block traffic a bit so you can pull out behind me."

"Okay."

He shoots me another killer smile and winks as he walks back to his squad. I wait for him to pull up alongside me. Traffic moves over a lane, and he slowly drives ahead of me so I can pull out behind him. I quickly do it. There's so much more traffic here than Duluth, Minnesota, where I'm from.

As soon as I'm behind him, he switches his lights off. I follow him a few blocks before he turns. A few blocks after that, he turns into a parking lot and leads me to Building Four. I turn into a parking place, and he backs his squad up so he's parked behind me. He gets out and smiles that incredible smile again. I have to catch my breath.

"Here you go. You're on the top floor. Right across the hall from me."

"Oh! You… live here, too?"

"Yep. You chose well. It's a good neighborhood. Crime rate is pretty low. People who live here are nice. They even have activities for residents. Every month they do something. Free coffee bar. Gym. Pool."

I smile shyly as I look up at him. He's so much taller than me. I'm only five feet three. His height helps him look so… dominant. Intimidating. I speak softly. "Choosing this place wasn't by chance."

"You researched it?" He grins as he looks down at me.

I nod. "I rarely do anything without thinking it through. Analyzing. Thinking through it more and harder."

7

"I see." He looks at my SUV. "So… you don't look like you have a lot of stuff. Do you have a moving truck coming?" He looks back down at me, and I look down at the ground and shake my head.

I gesture at the electric blue 2020 Ford Escape before looking back up. "This is it."

"Hmm… Well, if you'd like some help, I'm off in a couple hours. I'd be happy to."

"Oh! No, you've done so much already, Sergeant Chance. I don't have much."

"Matt. Please. Call me Matt." I nod and look down at the ground. "And what should I call you? Mysterious girl from Minnesota?"

I can't help but laugh a little. "Mariah. Yes, I'm from Minnesota. Duluth, actually. But you probably knew that since I'm sure you looked at and ran my plate."

He laughs. "Mariah from Duluth, Minnesota. Hand me your phone."

I look up at him completely confused. "Why?"

"I need your number so I can let you know when I'm on my way home, right?"

"Really. You don't need to. I can manage."

"I don't need to, but I want to. I wasn't giving you a choice. I'll bring a couple guys. We'll get it knocked out quickly. In the meantime, explore the grounds. Get your bearings." He holds out his hand. I shake my head and chuckle as I open the driver's side door and reach in to grab my phone. I hand it to him, and he quickly puts in his number and texts himself before handing it back to me.

"So… a couple hours?" I ask shyly.

"Yep." He shoots me another wink and another killer smile as he walks back to his squad. I watch as he drives away.

I shake my head, unsure of what just happened, as I reach into my SUV to grab a few necessities, my laptop included. I don't dare leave it in the Florida sun.

A few minutes later, after dropping my laptop and a few things in my new apartment, I do what Matt suggested and take a tour of the grounds. There's a nice pool. Fairly large. People seem to be enjoying it. I smile as I continue my walk. There's a nice walking trail behind the building. A park. People are running and walking on it. It's so different from Duluth. People seem happy here.

I find the coffee shop and the gym in the building. The gym is incredibly spacious with a lot of equipment. I continue up to my apartment and check my phone. I still have time before Matt is done with work.

It's the time that always kills me. Always forces me to think. And it's the thinking that always gets me.

Duluth is a long way away. My father is miles away. But I can't shut my mind off. I don't know if I made the right decision.

I moved to Gainesville, Florida, to start over. To get away from everyone and everything holding me back from reaching my full potential. I had very little support there. I don't here either, but at least I'll be doing it on my own terms. At least here, no one will be telling me I can't.

No one will be putting me down. No one will be making me feel like I'm not good enough or pretty enough. No one will make me feel like I'm not worth it ever again.

I take out my phone to text the one person in the world I know I can count on. Lyric Sharpe. She lives in the United Kingdom, but she's always here for me. I open my chat with her and smile to myself. She always brings me out of my moods.

Mariah: Just got to my apartment. Settling in. I had a bit of a breakdown getting here. Stupid GPS stopped working, and I got lost.

Lyric: Oh, good. I was worried. I hadn't heard from you in a while.

Mariah: I'm at the apartment thanks to a really hot cop who was really helpful. Turns out he lives across the hall from me.

Lyric: A hot cop, huh? You can't see it, but I'm smirking.

I laugh. Lyric is such a romantic. She knows I came here for a new start to my life, but I know she's plotting ways to get Matt and I together in her devious mind. She doesn't even know his name or anything about him, but she's already plotting.

Mariah: Pretty sure he's unavailable. He's too hot.

Lyric: Not necessarily. You don't know until you know. Don't close yourself off. Get to know him. He could be just what you need.

9

Mariah: He's so bossy. He's bringing a couple friends to help me move my stuff upstairs. He didn't give me an option. He totally just said he's doing it.

Lyric: Oh... my... God... You can't see it, but my eyes are so wide right now.

I look at my phone bewildered and shake my head. I'm not sure I want to know what just crossed her mind. Lyric could put me to shame with some of her thoughts. She says it's the British in her that makes her so wild. I just think she was born with a dirty mind.

Mariah: Dare I ask?

Lyric: I'm not saying a word. At least not right now! This is something you need to find out for yourself.

She sends me a bunch of emoji's. One is drooling. Another is blushing. There's also one that is red-faced, as if it's melting from the heat. She sends flames, and a bunch of blue hearts. There's even a few that are cry-laughing. And then she throws in an eggplant just because she can. I blush a furious shade of red that I'm sure doesn't have a name attached to it yet.

As I'm about to reply, I get another message. I look at it, and see a text from Matt. I feel myself smile before I can stop it.

Matt: Hey. Just leaving. I have a couple guys with me to help.

Mariah: Okay. Thank you for everything.

Matt: It's really no problem. We'll be there in a few minutes. I'll text. Meet us downstairs.

Mariah: Okay.

I go back to my conversation with Lyric.

Mariah: You're awful. Why are we friends again?

Lyric: Because I'm cute and adorable and awesome and annoying. And you love me for it all.

I crack up and wipe my eyes from the happy tears that have pooled in the corners of them, as I start making my way downstairs. A few moments later, she sends a couple of smug emojis as if she knew that she had made me laugh. That just makes me laugh harder.

Mariah: Is that why? And here I thought it was because you can make me laugh like no other.

Lyric: It could be that. There's no end of possibilities. I'm just so lovable!

10

Mariah: And perhaps a little arrogant.

Lyric: What? I'm clutching my chest in horror! There's not an arrogant bone in my body! I'm far too humble for that!

I reach my SUV and lean against it as I wait for Matt and his friends. True to his words, he arrives with two other people in tow as I'm wiping my eyes from the conversation with Lyric. I love that she can do that for me. Get me out of my own head. I quickly tell her that Matt and his friends have arrived as Matt strides up to me.

"Hey. Mariah? You okay?" He furrows his brows in concern.

"Hmm?" I look up at him confused, and then realize it looks like I'm crying. "Oh! Yeah. I was talking to a friend of mine. She had me laughing so hard, I was crying."

Matt nods, seemingly satisfied, as he gestures to his friends. "This is Brody and DJ. I work with them. Bribed them to help."

I laugh. "A cop bribing a cop? Sounds legit."

"He said there would be pizza," DJ says. He's a little taller than Matt. He's just as muscular. He's tall, dark, and ruggedly handsome, and I can't help but wonder if they grow attractive cops on the palm trees here.

"And beer," Brody says. He's shorter than both DJ and Matt. He's older and just starting to lose his light brown hair. His green eyes are as kind as his face. He's not as muscular as DJ and Matt, but I don't doubt he can hold his own.

"Did he now? Did he also tell you that I literally just moved here and have nothing in my refrigerator except one single water bottle?"

"He did. Minus the water bottle part," DJ jokes.

"I have beer at my place. And I'll order pizza. We have a pretty delicious local pizzeria here. Their pizza is to die for. Honestly. It's fantastic," Matt says.

I smile. "Well, okay then. I warn you, though. No furniture. We'll have to sit on the floor."

"We'll have the pizza at my place. My sister is bringing the kids. She should be there by the time we're done. She can bring the pizza with her."

"Kids?"

"Two beautiful girls and a boy." He beams at the thought of his kids. Where there are kids, there must be a wife or girlfriend. My smile falters, but I catch myself. Despite what I've told Lyric, I've given up on

11

love. I'm here for me. Not any kind of relationship. I need to go back to doing things on my own. Not be dependent on others. It only leads to heartbreak.

It takes less than an hour for the three of them to get everything from my SUV into my apartment. I look around. I have a lot less things than I thought, but I don't care. It's mine. This. It's just mine. It won't be messy. No one will be able to tell me I can't write or read whatever and whenever I want. It's all mine.

"Hey. Earth to Mariah."

I jump a little, then turn. Matt is standing so closely, and he smells so good. Like some kind of spicy, fresh, perfectly masculine scent. I have to force the immediate images that surge to my brain out of it. Images of me underneath him with his lips all over me are quickly pushed out of my head. He's taken. I have to remember he's taken, and I am not looking for love. Not even a little bit. Love is a bunch of shit.

"You seemed to be a million miles away."

"I may have been. Sorry."

"No need to apologize." He smiles softly. I give him a smile, but it's forced. He picks up on it immediately. Stupid cop instincts. "What's wrong?"

I look down. "Maybe I could have pizza with you guys another day?" I steel myself and look up at him.

His eyes. I love his deep brown eyes. But I won't let myself fall for him. He's taken. And I won't make the mistake of falling in love twice. I'll never fall in love again. Love is awful. It leads to nothing but heartbreak and misery. Years of it.

"What's going on?" His eyes are narrowed, and he folds his arms over his chest as he stands in front of me. "You have no furniture. No bed. You have no food. You were hardcore crying when I met you earlier. What are you running from?"

I swallow and shake my head. A lump forms instantly in my throat, and I fight back tears. "Nothing."

"Mariah." He reaches out a hand and touches my arm. It instantly soothes me, and that scares the hell out of me.

I'm not doing this.

I can't.

I won't.

12

I will never get close to a man again.

"I'm fine. I have a blanket and pillows until the stuff I ordered gets here."

"Let me at least bring you an air mattress."

I pull my arm away and walk to my bedroom. "Don't worry about me. I can take care of myself. I trust you can show yourself out." I snap at him and instantly feel bad about it, but I'm on the verge of a panic attack. I don't want him to see that. I need to be alone.

Finally, he moves to the door. "I don't take attitude very well."

Something clenches on my heart. I almost reach out for him, but stop myself. Instead, I bite my lip. "I'm sorry... I... didn't mean to snap."

He nods as he watches me for a moment. "I'm just across the hall, Mariah. If you need me, don't hesitate."

I wait until the door closes before I burst into tears again. I grab my pillows and blankets and make a makeshift bed that I curl up in.

My mind immediately goes crazy thinking of everything all at once. I'm divorced. I have no family. Nothing. My father hates me. I'm starting completely over in a completely new city. I don't know anyone. There's no way I'll succeed on my own. I've never been totally alone before. Even though I got where I am on my own, I've never been totally alone. My mind races out of control with all the reasons why I can't do this.

My chest tightens, and I fight to breathe as I curl up on the floor in my new bedroom. I reach for my phone and start texting Lyric. She's the only one who has ever been able to talk me down. She has anxiety herself and knows how to deal with me and my panic attacks. She knows how to get me out of my head. She's always known just what to say.

Despite the constant texting, messaging, and talking, I can't calm down. Nothing is helping.

My mind continues to race long into the night, and I fight wave after wave of nausea. Panic attack after panic attack until I feel like I won't make it through until the morning.

This was a mistake.

A big mistake.

I'll never be able to do this on my own.

I'm thirty-eight, and I have never been able to survive on my own. I've always had help. I've always had someone to lean on. I have no one here. All I have is a phone connecting me to the one person who has ever had hope for me and confidence in me.

But she was wrong.

I'm failing her right now.

I'm failing everyone.

Chapter Two

☆ Matt ☆

I've been lying in bed for hours unable to sleep. I can't get Mariah's beautiful golden hazel eyes out of my head. I love how they look like such a deep blue one second, then green the next. Just as soon as I think I figure them out, they turn gray with these incredible gold flecks. Her sexy smile won't leave me alone. Her incredible mystery both intrigues and throws me into a rollercoaster ride of confusion.

I know she's hiding something. I felt it when I first saw her crying. I had been passing by on my usual patrol when I saw her hunched over her steering wheel. At first I thought maybe she'd passed out behind the wheel. It was hot out earlier. It felt like it was in the nineties. It isn't unusual seeing the heat fuck with people like that. It wasn't until after I pulled up behind her and walked to her window that I saw her entire body shaking with uncontrollable sobs.

When she looked at me, tears streaking her face, my heart broke for her.

I'd already run her plate when I pulled up. I knew her name. Her age. It wasn't until after I left her alone in her apartment that I had decided I needed to know more about her. So I kicked DJ and Brody out, leaving my twelve-year-old nephew to watch his younger siblings for about an hour. I drove back to Headquarters and ran a check on her. I didn't have much to go on, but I found out she'd been married. Maybe twice. Her maiden name wasn't Carter.

It was Peterson. After that it was Brinsley. And now it is Carter. I'd decided to run a check on marriage licenses for her, but my Captain had come in. I didn't want to get caught running unauthorized shit, so I went home with more questions about this girl than answers.

Regardless, she's beautiful, and I can't get her out of my head. I'd only gotten her to share a little bit with me, but she did say she's a writer. Must be unpublished, though, because I can't find shit she's written anywhere. Under any of her names.

I growl at my thoughts, willing them away so I can at least attempt to sleep, but the Gods above are not on my side. I hear a knock on my door.

Glancing at the clock, I growl again. Who the fuck could possibly think it's a good idea to show up here at three in the morning?

I don't bother with a shirt, but I do throw a pair of sweats on. I might be pissed off, but I have a little dignity at the very least.

I open my door a little more forcefully than I intended and see Mariah standing on the other side. She's crying and looks like she's fighting to breathe as she hugs herself in the hallway. Her cellphone is clutched tight in her hand. Her skimpy short blue shorts and barely there tank top do unthinkable things to me, and I force myself to focus on anything other than how her pajamas hug her every curve and leave nothing about her cup size to the imagination.

"Holy shit. What happened? Are you okay?" I let my cop instincts take over, and I quickly look down each side of the hallway looking for anyone who could have hurt her.

She shakes her head as she lets out a sob, then covers her mouth to try and hold back another one as she attempts a few deep breaths. She fails miserably.

"Mariah, what happened?" I had been fighting against pulling her inside, but I give up. I gently take her hand and tug her into my apartment.

"I..."

16

"Mariah? Are you okay? Did he answer?" I look down at her phone. She's staring blankly at it, like she isn't registering it's in her hand or that anyone is talking.

I close the door, keeping her hand in mine. She's gripping it so tightly that I'm convinced she's afraid she'll drown if she lets go.

"Mariah?" I gently reach for the phone and slowly take it from her hand. "Mariah? Who's on the phone?" She doesn't answer. Her eyes are filled to the brim with tears that haven't started falling yet.

"Hello? If you can hear me, my name's Lyric."

I bring the phone to my ear. "Lyric? It's Matt. Give me an idea of what's happening."

"She can't calm down. She's having a really rough night. Panic attack. One of her worst. I've been trying to calm her for hours now. Nothing has worked. I can't talk her down this time. I knew I needed help, and remembered her telling me you lived in the apartment across from her. She said you helped her move in. So I talked her into going to you."

"Okay. I've got her. You going to be okay? Can I have her call you tomorrow?"

"Don't worry about me. I'm okay now that she's with you. Just have her message. I live in the United Kingdom. I don't want to know how much this call is costing her. And Matt? Make sure she does message. Or I'll find a way to kick your ass from here. I may be small, but I can still kick ass."

I can't help but chuckle as I watch Mariah closely. "I'm glad she has you, sweetheart. I'll have her message." I say goodbye, not taking my eyes off Mariah. I slip her cellphone into the pocket of my sweats.

Letting her keep her grip on my hand, I reach up and tuck her hair behind her ear, leaving my hand on her cheek. I look deeply into her eyes, trying to will her to trust me. Her beautiful golden hazel eyes are wild and unfocused. They're darting around like she's expecting a demon to jump out and attack her at any second. "Mariah... What caused this, beautiful?"

She sniffles and continues to try and hold back her sobs. "I..."

"What the fuck happened to you to cause this, honey?" I pull her into my chest, holding her close as I lead her towards my bedroom.

"Matt?" My ten year old niece pops out of my guest bedroom. I glance at her, but keep focused on Mariah. "Are you going to work?"

"No. It's okay, sweetie. Go back to bed."

"I'm thirsty."

"Go get some water from the bathroom and go back to bed, Brit." She hurries to the bathroom. I hear the water running and a few moments later, Brit sleepily walks back to the room. "Mariah. Honey, look at me. Focus on me. Come on. You can do it."

"I... shouldn't... have... bothered... you." She's near hyperventilation.

"Stop that. I told you if you needed me, I'm here. I meant it." Keeping a strong grip on her hand, I walk her into my bedroom. She hesitates in the doorway, so I look down at her. "I don't want to wake the kids. The bathroom is between my room and theirs, so if you need to cry you can without the fear of waking them up. You can trust me, Mariah. I just want to help you."

She nods as I lead her to my bed, closing the door behind us. I sit and tug her down next to me. Her death grip on my hand has only managed to get tighter. I'd let her break it if that's what she needs right now.

With my free hand, I tuck her hair behind her ear once more. I keep my voice low and as calming as I possibly can. "Talk to me. I want to help, but I can't do that if you don't talk to me. Tell me what you need from me right now."

"I can't... calm down."

"Mariah. I can see that. Tell me what you need. Please?"

"I'm having... a panic attack. It... won't stop." She's shaking and trembling.

"I know you're having a panic attack, honey. What I don't know is what you need from me." I don't want to be forceful with her or make an attempt at talking her through it and it be the wrong thing to do.

She shakes her head again and starts sobbing. "I don't know." She hides her face in her free hand, and I make a decision. Unlike most people I've seen having a panic attack, she seems to need closeness.

I nod. "Okay."

I crawl into my bed and pull her in next to me. I gently untangle her death grip on my hand so I can hold her tightly and with both arms. She releases her grip on my hand and immediately finds anything else she can grab onto. I'm not wearing a shirt so she grabs the waistband of my sweats.

"Shit." I whisper the word into her hair as I inhale sharply. She's dangerously close to grabbing my cock, but I force myself to ignore my body's immediate and physical reaction to her. Now is not the time. "Mariah. Listen to me." I whisper the words in her ear. "I want you to focus on me, sweetheart. Focus on my breathing. Be a good girl and focus on me. You can do that for me, right?"

She nods. "I…" Her long, dark brown hair and her silky smooth skin smells like coconut.

"Take deep breaths with me."

"I… can't. I can't." She shakes her head.

"Shh… You can. Do it now. Ready?" I take a deep breath as I run my fingers through her hair. She tries to, but it's unsteady.

"I can't."

"Shh... You can, honey. Focus on me. Just me. Another breath." I take another deep breath. She inhales, but coughs. I hug her as tightly as I can against me.

"Can't."

"You can, honey. Feel me. Feel me breathing. Breathe with me. We're doing this together, okay? Be a good girl. You and me."

She puts her head against my chest. "You and me."

"You and me, Mariah. Feel me breathing, and breathe with me."

She shakily lets go of the waistband of my sweats and softly moves her hand up to my chest. I keep my breathing steady for her. I know she needs it.

"Distract me."

I smile into her hair and chuckle. "I can think of a lot of ways to distract you, and none of them are appropriate."

She gives me a shaky laugh. "Tell me a story."

I feel her start to relax as I hold her tightly to me. "Once upon a time there was a princess named Jasmine."

She shakes her head. "Aladdin is one of my favorite Disney fairytales, but I meant like a funny story. Something that happened to you on patrol or something."

I smile into her hair as I continue running my fingers through it. She continues becoming calmer. "I know what you meant." Her shaky hand on my chest snakes around my waist. "Improvement."

She chuckles and shifts so she's as close to me as she can get. "A little. Please tell me a story?"

"Three years ago, I was on patrol. I got a call about a fight that had broken out a few streets down from where I was. I took the call. A couple other squads responded. When we got there, there were a ton of kids in the street. Ten. Maybe twelve. All covered in different colored paints. Blue. Green. Purple. Red. You name it. They were having a paint balloon fight. The person who called it in was an older lady. Hated noise."

"Sounds right."

I tangle my fingers in her hair and start comfortingly rubbing her neck. "Yeah, she's the neighborhood complainer. As my partner, DJ, was talking to her, a couple other cops including myself had joined in with the kids. Next thing DJ knows, we had turned everyone against him. Every single one of us threw a balloon in his direction. He got hit maybe ten times. The woman who called went ballistic because some of the spray from the balloons exploding against his back hit her." I continue running my fingers through her hair. She chuckles again as her breathing continues to regulate. "She made a complaint against the three of us. The Chief of Police, instead of reprimanding us, took our dash cam videos and used it as community police training. Which means -"

"Police and the community building a partnership. In simple terms."

I look at her, a little surprised. "Yeah, exactly."

She smiles against my chest. "I went to school for Law Enforcement. I have a Master's in Criminal Justice with a corrections concentration. I also have a Bachelor's in both Legal Studies and Criminal Justice and my AA in Law Enforcement. And just because I'm not complex enough, I threw in a diploma in Broadcasting because I felt like it."

"Wow. That's... truly amazing. And you're a writer?"

I feel her smile against my chest. "Of romance novels. Go figure, right? By the time I graduated and did my internship, I was so turned off to Law Enforcement in general. Not because I hate the profession. It's just that I wanted to feel like I was doing more to help people. All I felt was that I would be showing up to the same house over and over again and no one would really be getting helped. I wanted more. And the idea of being a cop sent anxiety I didn't even really know I had into overdrive. I mean, I

20

knew I had it. But I'd always been able to fight it. The older I get, the less I'm able to fight. And the more weak and childish I feel."

"That doesn't make you weak or childish. You fighting through this makes you strong as hell."

I can feel her smile against my chest. "Thank you for saying that."

I hug her a little tighter. "What about your writing? Are you published?"

"I have a couple of books out. Under my first and middle name. Mariah Marie."

That explains why I couldn't find her. I'll have to look her books up.

She takes a deep breath and tries to sit up, but my arms tighten around her. "I know you aren't ready for me to let go. You're still shaky, Mariah."

"I'll be okay. Really. I'm so sorry I bothered you."

"Stop. Stop. I'm not letting you go until I'm confident you'll be okay. And right now, I know you won't be. I can feel how freaked out you are. I know if I let you go, it'll send you right back into another one." I'm far more in tune to her than I care to admit, but I'm not kidding around. If I'm what she needs to calm down, so be it.

"Why are you being so nice to me? You don't even know me."

"I don't need to know you to know you need me. I know I'm your anchor right now. So forget about getting up. Maybe in the morning you'll trust me enough to tell me what happened to you, honey. For now, just relax. Keep feeling me breathe and breathe with me." She does what I tell her to. "Good girl. We're getting through this night, okay? You aren't alone. It's you and me, honey."

She slowly nods and then whispers to me. "You and me."

I rub my hand slowly up and down her back and keep my other tangled in her satiny hair. Her breathing begins to even out, and I feel the very moment she falls asleep safe in my arms. I don't know what the fuck happened to this girl, but no fucking way is it ever going to happen again. Not on my watch.

Exhausted after Mariah finally falls asleep, I close my eyes and fall asleep right after her, still holding her tightly in my arms.

21

Chapter Three

☆ Mariah ☆

I wake up confused. I'm surrounded by a spicy, intoxicating scent that is so comforting that all I want to do is never leave wherever it is that I am.

I look around the room I'm in. It's clean. Spacious. The walls are a deep blue. The dresser and nightstand all match the oak of the bedframe.

The bed is the most comfortable bed I've ever been in. The white sheets are so soft, and I never want to get out from under the blue comforter I'm under.

I must be dreaming.

I don't have any furniture yet. My bed is supposed to be delivered today. My chairs and couches? All with the bed.

So where the hell am I?

I slowly sit up.

I feel like I got hit by a truck. My chest is killing me. I clutch my chest as everything comes back to me at once.

The panic attack.

The fear.

Lyric.

Matt.

I whip my head to the bed, holding my hand to my head at the dizziness the movement causes, but Matt isn't in it. There is, however, a note on the table. I quickly reach over and grab it.

Hey, honey.

I don't want you to wake up and start panicking again. I wanted you to know where I am. I had to take the kids to school. I'll be back about nine. Traffic can be a little tough around the school. Please stay in bed until I get back. You had a really rough night, and I would feel a lot better if you didn't go back to your place right now. At least until I have a second to make sure you're okay. Don't forget to message Lyric. She was really worried last night. And I wouldn't want her to go through with her threat of kicking my ass. She sounds like she'd be scrappy.

Yours,
Matt

I raise an eyebrow at his sign off. "Mine?"

Feeling weak after a night of attack after attack, I do as he says and lay back down, glancing at the clock on his nightstand. "Almost nine. He'll probably be back before I have a chance to sneak out anyway."

I burrow back under the comforter and breathe in Matt's incredibly calming scent. I don't even care that he's taken. I'm lucky his girlfriend wasn't here last night. Maybe they don't live together.

Regardless, I may be pretty sure I've fucked up my entire life, but the one thing I'm grateful for is Lyric's decision to push me into coming over here last night. She was right. I didn't even have to ask him to help me. He just did it. And I don't even know how. No one but Lyric has ever been able to calm me down like he did. Just being near him helped considerably, but knowing I wasn't alone… God, that was everything.

Everything.

I find my cellphone on Matt's dresser and open up my chat with Lyric. I hate when she worries about me. It always causes her to panic a little, even though she doesn't say anything. She would rather stay silent than risk worrying me. That's just how she is.

Mariah: Hi. I just wanted to let you know I'm okay. You were right. Matt helped. A lot.

She answers almost right away. Like she was waiting for me to message her. I smile weakly.

Lyric: I'm so glad.

Mariah: You didn't sleep, did you?

Lyric: I refuse to answer that on the basis that it can incriminate me. So... No comment.

Mariah: I knew it. Lyric...

Lyric: Okay. I slept a little. But only because by that time exhaustion took over, and I had no choice. I'll be fine. I don't have much to do today, so I can take a nap later.

I tell Lyric to take a nap as I hear the front door open. I immediately sit up. The quickness of my movement, though, makes me dizzy as hell, and I immediately feel nauseated. I hold my head still and close my eyes. I breathe slowly, deeply, waiting for the feeling to pass.

Almost instantaneously, I feel strong arms encircle me and pull me close. "You okay?"

"Um... I sat up too fast. I went dizzy and felt a little nauseous."

His scent.

Him.

It's like magic. Everything stops. The dizziness. The nausea. Gone.

I bury my head in his chest and grip his shirt. I feel my cheeks flush and I take a few deep breaths as I try to steady myself.

"How do you do it?"

"Do what?"

"Calm me down. Almost instantly?"

He hums into my hair, his chest vibrating and tickling my cheek. "Maybe it's fate."

"Fate's a fickle bitch, and she's never been kind to me. I don't see that changing any time soon."

He laughs. "Then divine intervention. Call it whatever you want, but I was in the right place at the right time. You needed me. I was there. And going forward? You need me, I'll be there."

I don't know if I can believe that. Especially since I know he has a significant other. But he's here now, and I'll take what I can get. I feel his

24

fingers tangle in my hair, and I involuntarily melt into him. What is wrong with me? Why does he make me feel this way?

"Tell me what happened, Mariah. What the hell scared you so bad that you ended up in the state you were in?"

Tears sting my eyes, and I pull back from him. "I can't, Matt." I wipe a tear away and start to get up.

Matt grabs my hand. "Please don't run away."

I look at his hand on mine. Part of me wants to run. Far. And as fast as I can. The other part really feels connected to him. Wants me to open up to him. To bring down my walls. Like I can trust him.

"Rih, please talk to me."

Rih. No one has ever called me Rih.

It's new. I like it. But mostly I like it when he says it.

I shake my head and gently pull away from him as I get out of the bed. I can't get attached to someone again. Especially someone who is unavailable.

He follows. I knew he would. I didn't want him to.

Or maybe I did. I don't know. I don't know much of anything right now.

"Thank you, Matt. For everything."

"Rih. You can trust me." He reaches out to touch my cheek, and I lean into his hand briefly. I really think I can.

"I know."

"Then talk to me. Tell me what happened."

I shake my head again, and I reach up to take his hand in mine. I give it a light squeeze before I turn to leave.

"Mariah, I can't help you if you don't let me in."

I pause by his front door and turn to him once more. "But you have. What you've already done for me is so much more than what anyone but Lyric has ever done for me."

He gently takes my arm. "I'll wait if that's what you need. I'll wait for as long as it takes." He tucks my hair behind my ear. "You can trust me."

I give him a soft smile. "I know."

And that's what scares me so much. Trusting. Knowing I can trust him. I trusted a man before. And it backfired on me, in one of the worst

25

ways possible. I ended up getting hurt. I refuse to let that happen again. I can't let it happen again. I don't think I'd survive it a second time.

I make the mistake of looking up into his eyes. The kindness there, the protectiveness, it makes me want to tell him everything. I can see the moment he realizes he has me.

"Tell me," he says once more.

I sigh. "My ex. My dad. I fled Duluth for a lot of reasons. But they were the biggest. I was married to my ex for almost ten years." I decide to open up a little, but I'm really not sure how much I should. "There were a lot of reasons that went into the divorce. But I think the biggest was the way he treated me. He wasn't physically abusive. But he was mentally. He was always making me feel like I wasn't good enough. And the really sad thing is... I..." I tilt my head a little and give a sad smile. "I don't think he really knew everything he was doing. I don't think he was really capable of comprehending it fully. It was hard to walk away because I don't think he meant it."

He shakes his head and runs his thumb over my lip. "I think everyone has the ability to make a choice. And I think all of our responses and actions are reliant upon the choices those others make. Whatever it was that he did to you, I don't doubt you made the choice that was best for you in leaving."

I smile softly. "I don't really doubt that I needed to leave. What I doubt is the way I did it. I know how hurt he is. He cried the whole time. And I feel like a truly horrible person because of it. And there's also my dad. He's a long story. A story for another day."

I jump at the knock on his door behind me. He gives my arm a soft squeeze as he reaches around me to open it. I turn and see DJ standing on the other side.

"Hey there, honey. Please tell me you just tamed our asshole of a Sergeant. He really needs to get laid." DJ gives him a teasing smile. I look at him astonished he would say something like that when Matt has a significant other.

Matt's eyes nearly pop out of his head, and his face turns red. I bite back a laugh, though I know he's pissed.

"What the fuck is wrong with you?" Matt asks. "Why are you here?"

"Because Mariah didn't answer her door. I took a chance and came here hoping she fucked the jerk out of you so you stop terrorizing the department."

"Wait. Wait. I... thought..." I look up at Matt. "Don't you have a girlfriend? Or wife or something?"

"What?" His eyes register the confusion I feel. "I'm not seeing anyone, and I've never been married."

"But... your kids..."

DJ chuckles. "Matt doesn't have kids. He's too much of a dick. Those are his sister's kids."

I have no idea why my heart suddenly feels like it has wings and is trying to fly out of my chest. The butterflies I didn't know existed in my stomach take flight. I don't know whether the feeling I'm feeling is nausea, or if I'm stupidly in love. That's always been my problem. It's how I got in trouble to begin with. I fall in love far too fast. Lyric says it's the romance writer in me. That I'm a hopeless romantic. I keep telling her she's crazy, but I know she's right.

Matt shakes his head and focuses back on DJ. "Now that we got that bullshit out of the way, what the hell are you knocking on Mariah's door at nine in the morning for?"

"Alright. Alright. Seriously. I was worried about her." He looks at me. The concern shining in his eyes is a little shocking. Besides Lyric and now Matt, I don't think I've ever seen anyone look at me that concerned before.

"I'm okay," I say a little shyly and a lot taken aback.

"Good. I was a little worried with how quickly you decided you weren't hungry and wanted to be alone."

"I... was having a hard time... adjusting, I guess. I had a pretty bad night. Matt..." I look up at him, not really sure how to describe what he did for me, and how much he helped me. "I..."

Matt takes over as he sees me struggling to find the words. "She was having a really bad night. She turned up at my door late, around three in the morning. She had spent most of the night trying to get through it with the help of her friend Lyric, but Lyric could only do so much on text and chat and the phone. She's from the UK. So she convinced her to come to me for help. She remembered Mariah telling her that I lived in the apartment across from her. That I had told her I'm here if she needs me."

27

DJ doesn't hesitate to hug me, and for some ridiculous reason, I feel safe. Like I had with Matt. I find myself sinking into the embrace, comforted.

He lets go, and I immediately miss his embrace. I didn't realize how much I needed it until he let go. "Give me your phone. I want you to have my phone number, too. Just in case Matt isn't here."

"Good idea. That way if this happens again and I'm working, you have someone you can get in touch with."

"Wait... don't you work together?" I look between the two of them.

"DJ is also a Sergeant, but he works where he's needed."

DJ shakes his head at my confused expression. "My shifts can be day or mid or overnight. It depends where they need help. I try to keep a regular schedule, but sometimes it doesn't work that way. I always get my hours. Sometimes I get more. I like it this way. Gives me the opportunity to work with as many other officers as I can. Get to know more people in the community. Make more contacts because I work in different parts of the city."

"That sounds complicated," I say, shaking my head slightly.

"It's really not bad."

I smile softly and nod. "Um... I really should get home. I have the delivery people coming with my stuff. I have to get some things put away before they get there. And I have to get the laptop set up for when Lyric calls. She wants to be online when the furniture is delivered. She's protective like that. She will most likely help me place the furniture, too."

"Stay for breakfast," Matt says, his eyes burning into mine.

I sigh and shake my head. "My stomach is really upset, Matt. Really. I appreciate all of this." I look at DJ. "And I really appreciate you coming and checking on me. It was so thoughtful." I take a deep breath. "I'm just really not feeling well. I need to regroup. But I promise I'll check in. I won't hide myself away. I just really need the time by myself."

Matt narrows his eyes. I smile once more, giving both of their arms a gentle squeeze, and walk to my own apartment. I close my door softly behind me and lean against it, closing my eyes.

Trusting anyone would mean letting down my carefully constructed walls. I spent years building them up. Years becoming the tough girl that my ex and my father spent years tearing down. If not for those walls, I wouldn't have gotten divorced last month. I wouldn't have left.

I'd still be in Minnesota letting him make me feel like I'm not worthy. Letting my dad pull me into his psychotic orbit.

I can't.

I can't let myself trust. He'll only hurt me like everyone else has.

Unfortunately, I don't think I have a choice. Both DJ and Matt have managed to make me feel like I can trust them.

I take a deep breath and push away from the door. I walk to my bedroom and start picking up my blankets. I move methodically throughout my apartment and push boxes against the wall to make room for my delivery.

Hard as I may try, I can't get Matt out of my head. I can't get the way his smooth chest and rock hard abs felt against me. How his powerful arms made me feel safer than I have ever felt in my life. I can't get over how he wouldn't let me go until he felt that I was okay. How he held me until I fell asleep. How he was so careful to not wake me up when he left.

Of course I would fall for someone when I'm trying not to.

It doesn't matter anyway. I didn't come here to fall in love. Love is for fools. And I refuse to be a fool ever again.

Ever.

Again.

Chapter Four

☆ Matt ☆

I'm not letting Mariah shut down on me. Not after all the progress I made getting her to open up last night. Not after all she told me this morning about her ex... The hints she dropped about her dad. I'm not letting her backtrack. I'll push and push until she understands she can trust me.

I knock on her door. I've given her three hours. I know she gets furniture delivered today because she said she was. And I know she hasn't eaten because it's unlikely she's left her apartment if she's waiting for her delivery. I also haven't heard her door. And I am not ashamed for a second to say I've been listening. She hasn't left. And no one has delivered anything to her.

I don't know why I feel so strongly towards her. I don't know why I feel like she needs me, or why I feel like I have to be there. I'm thirty-nine years old, and I've never felt like this. I've dated. I've had significant relationships. Other than my nieces and nephew and my family, I have never felt the overwhelming need to be a protector towards anyone. The fiercest of protectors.

"You sure she's not going to bite your head off? I bet she has a mean streak if you piss her off," DJ says.

I had decided to bring her lunch and help with furniture after the delivery got there. DJ decided he was going to help, too. I didn't try to stop him. I can tell he's feeling the same type of protective instinct as I am towards her. I'm grateful about it because it means that he'll be just as much of an impenetrable wall as I will be. I wouldn't have been able to keep him away if I wanted to.

After a few moments, Mariah opens the door. Just as I suspected, she hasn't changed out of her pajamas. She hasn't put anything away. Only moved boxes against the wall to make room for the furniture.

"We brought lunch." I already know she'll try to stop us from entering her apartment, and I'm not playing games, so I walk past her and put the bags on the counter. DJ follows dropping a kiss to her head. The shock registering on her face is sexy as fuck.

"Matt.... DJ... You guys didn't have to. I'm really not hun-"

"Hungry?" I turn to her and cross my arms over my chest. "When was the last time you ate? Because I know you didn't eat dinner last night. And you sure as hell didn't stay for breakfast with me. You haven't left your apartment. You have no food in here. So I'm gonna guess, and you tell me how hot or cold I am. Sound good, beautiful?" I look intensely down at her. She looks up at me, mouth slightly open in pure shock. "Yesterday morning. I'll bet you stopped at a gas station and decided on a donut."

"H-how do you...? I mean..." She shakes her head, and I grin, still standing with my back against the counter; my arms folded over my chest. She's adorable when she blushes. "No. I mean... No. How do you know I didn't go shopping?" I raise an eyebrow. DJ, standing against the counter across from me, turns and opens her fridge. It holds nothing but a half a bottle of Dasani. "Okay. Fine. I haven't gone shopping, but you don't know I didn't order anything from somewhere to eat."

I nod as he closes the refrigerator and goes back to his position with his back against the counter and arms over his chest, mimicking me. "I don't see any takeout containers anywhere. No evidence of you eating a damn thing. So either you're the cleanest fucking person in the entire history of humanity and already took your garbage out, or you haven't eaten."

31

She glares at me, and I flash her a cocky grin. "I could've thrown it out already."

"But you didn't. Because you haven't left the apartment."

"I could've."

"You didn't." I turn and start taking out the food, arranging it on the counter.

"I didn't know what kind of sandwich you like so I guessed," DJ says. "I got you Turkey and Swiss. I didn't put anything on it. I got all the vegetables and stuff on the side."

I take out containers with lettuce, tomatoes, pickles, olives, and peppers. Mayo and mustard packets. Ranch. "DJ also got soup. The loaded potato soup is really good. Also, he didn't know what you like to drink so he just grabbed a couple waters. If you want something else, I might have it. I can grab it from my place."

"Uh… Matt, I don't… I have nowhere to sit."

I glance at her, then nod to the room in front of us. "Looks like you have a floor. And there's a pretty inviting balcony right there."

"You're truly impossible. Do you know that?"

"He's an asshole. You can say it," DJ says with a smile.

I grin and shrug. "Asshole for sure. But I prefer determined."

She shakes her head and smiles. "Fine. Determined. I'll give you that."

"That's my girl." I don't miss the second look of surprise she gives me at calling her my girl. She recovers pretty quickly and focuses on building her sandwich. I watch as she puts mayo on it followed by tomato, pickle, and black olives. She leaves the lettuce, peppers, and mustard.

"Not a lettuce, pepper, or mustard fan?" I ask. She's quiet as we settle on the floor. I sit across from her so I can watch her. DJ sits next to her.

"I don't do well with peppers or spicy things. Sometimes… pepper is too hot for me. Lettuce upsets my stomach and makes me physically sick. I don't know why. I like mustard, but not on sandwiches like this. I prefer honey Dijon, but on very rare occasions. I don't eat it a lot." She keeps her eyes focused on her sandwich and soup.

I smile. "I'll remember for next time."

She takes a small bite of the sandwich, then looks up at me. "Next time?"

32

"Yes, next time."

She smiles and nods, and we all fall silent a few minutes as we eat. It's like she's trying to process the possibility of a next time, but she's too scared to let herself think it could happen. Finally, she looks up at me and starts talking. Her voice is low and soft, and I almost have to strain to hear her.

"Um... If you're serious about a next time, my favorite sandwich is roasted chicken. Sometimes I like bacon added. And I just like the meat warmed up. I don't like the sandwich toasted."

I smile at her as I nod. "Okay. I'll remember. For next time."

"There's going to be a lot more of this, Mariah. You're too fun to be around for me to leave you alone," DJ says, leaning into her side and nudging her before sitting back up. I shoot him a grateful look.

I want her to understand that I'm not going anywhere. That DJ isn't. That she has a friend in him. That she has me. As crazy as it sounds, even to myself, I can't leave her be. I wouldn't be able to walk away at this point if I tried to. The feel of her in my arms last night, in my bed, despite the situation...

Fuck me, but it felt like the most natural thing in the world. Like she belonged there. It felt right.

"Rih. Tell me what happened last night," I say.

"We know that what you did tell him isn't everything. There has to be more to it than that."

She smiles softly and focuses on finishing her soup. Just when I think she's finally going to open up, her buzzer sounds. She looks up at it almost sadly. "I'm sorry. That's probably the delivery people."

"Go. We'll clean up, baby."

She looks at me in surprise and confusion again, and I shoot her a grin as she gets up to answer the intercom. Yep, throwing her off guard is my new favorite thing to do.

DJ and I quickly gather everything off the floor and bring it to the counter where I left the bag. Mariah looks far more relaxed than she did, but there's still a sadness behind her eyes. A fear that I don't like. Especially since I think her fear is directed at me a little bit.

I really don't like that.

I glance over at Mariah's open laptop as it dings and raise an eyebrow. Mariah, standing by her door waiting for the delivery, reaches for the laptop, but DJ beats her to it.

"I got it. You wait for them," he says.

"It's Lyric. I told her when they said they would arrive. She wanted to be online with me in case they tried something. I guess she doesn't need to be since you guys are here." I watch as she nervously bites at the inside of her cheek.

I chuckle. "Mariah, if you want Lyric on video, she'll be on video."

DJ answers the Skype call. "Hey -" His eyes widen, and he cuts himself off. I lean over his shoulder to see the woman who just made him speechless.

I'll admit, she's gorgeous. Her chestnut brown hair lays in waves over her shoulders. Her wide-eyes are a hazel color, sort of like Mariah's except the opposite end of the spectrum. Depending on how the light hits them, they look brown, green, or even gray. She's a beautiful woman. There's no denying that.

"Hey, you must be Lyric," I say with a friendly smile. "I'm Matt."

"Hey, Matt. Nice to put a face to the name," she says softly. I don't miss for a second that her eyes never leave DJ's, but I take the opportunity to get a little revenge on him for this morning.

"This… is DJ," I say, patting him on the back. "Usually he's a little more polite, but apparently he forgot how to speak around beautiful women."

DJ shakes his head, like he's coming out of a daze, and looks at me. "Asshole."

Lyric cracks up. "Thank you! I needed that." She tilts her head, looking DJ up and down, and licks her lip with a slow smirk. "I bet you I'll have a lot of fun with you in my dreams tonight. Well… that's if you could handle a woman like me…" She trails off with a wicked smile.

It's like he suddenly remembers who he is. He gives her a slow, arrogant smile and puts on his best Southern accent. "I have no doubt I could handle a woman like you. I believe in conserving water, but something tells me you and I would be using a lot of it."

She gives him a slow smile, a little unsure of his train of thought. I bite my lip because I've known him long enough to know exactly where he's going. "And why's that?"

"Because we'd never be able to get clean enough with everything I'd be doing to you." He smiles wider. She nearly chokes as she inhales sharply and lowers her eyes submissively. "Well, damn...," he says, seeing exactly what I did. She's a submissive. And considering DJ is a dominant, she's definitely appealing to him on every level. "I may have to hop on the next flight and bring you home."

"She does plan on moving here," Mariah says from the door, amused.

Lyric's face turns red as she looks up at him through her lashes and bites her lip. "Maybe you should..."

"Keep looking at me through those sexy, submissive eyes of yours..."

Lyric quickly looks down. I wink at the screen and glance at Mariah. She's shaking her head, but she's smiling. A few minutes later, everything is picked up and put away, and the delivery guys are bringing in Mariah's furniture. She's standing next to me in the kitchen, trying to stay out of their way.

"Which room is the bed going, Miss?" the delivery guy asks.

"Oh. Um... The first one. Where the dresser is."

I watch as the delivery guy's eyes travel up and down her body. Her pajamas don't leave much to the imagination, but I don't care. I glare at him and grab her around the waist, pulling her into me while DJ and Lyric talk over Skype. My protective instincts take immediate control. "Problem?"

"Nope. No, sir."

"Good. Finish this delivery and stop staring at her. She's taken."

His eyes go wide. He flushes with embarrassment as he quickly walks away. DJ and Lyric both stare in open-mouthed shock. Mariah waits for him to disappear from sight before she turns around and swats me in the chest.

"Seriously? Taken? What the hell?"

I grab her wrists and glare down at her. "Tell me you didn't like that guy."

"What if I did?" I continue to glare and finally she breaks. "Fine. I didn't. His staring did make me uncomfortable." My gaze softens as the delivery guys leave for another load. As soon as they're gone, I release her wrists. "Thank you for pretending."

"I wasn't pretending."

She stares at me with wide owl eyes. "What?"

"I wasn't pretending, Mariah. As far as I'm concerned, you became mine as soon as I saw you crying in your vehicle."

"U… um..." Her eyes dart to Lyric's, and I hide the smile fighting to surface.

The confusion she expected to find with Lyric isn't there. Instead, Lyric and DJ are both smiling widely, like they know something she doesn't. Mariah, bewildered, focuses her attention on the chaos of the delivery drivers. I wait for the delivery people to leave her apartment for another load.

"I'll be right back."

"What? Um… Okay, I guess."

I bend down and kiss her cheek, surprising her again. "I'll be right back," I repeat.

I quickly make my way to my apartment and to my bedroom. I grab one of my t-shirts and hurry back to her, handing her the t-shirt.

"I have my own t-shirts."

"Did you notice how many of those guys were ogling you?" She bites her lip and looks at the ground. I grab the t-shirt and put it over her head. "Trust me, Rih. Guys don't typically fuck with women they know belong to someone else."

She sighs and puts it on the rest of the way. She nearly drowns in it, but I've never seen anything more beautiful in my life. Something about her in my SWAT t-shirt is sexy as hell.

The delivery guys bring in the last chair and a table. Mariah signs for her stuff.

"Do you need us to put your bed together, Miss?"

Man, this asshole doesn't take a hint. He steps closer to her, and she backs right into me. I put my arm possessively around her. "We got it. Thanks. We can put *our* bed together on our own. See?" I gesture to DJ. "Even brought myself a little help and everything."

"Sure thing." He smiles and winks at her, and she steps even closer to me. He leaves with everyone else, but I wait a couple of seconds before I let her go.

"I'm really sorry. I didn't mean to do that, but that guy really freaked me out. I don't really even know why. It's not like I can't handle myself."

"Glad I was here to help you out then."

"Really glad you were there," Lyric mumbles. "If I could figure out how to come through this screen, I would've kicked that guy in his hairy old man balls."

DJ roars with laughter. "Fuck, I'm using that!"

I chuckle and kiss the top of Mariah's head. I could spend my life kissing her and never get sick of it. "I have to pick up the kids in a couple hours. My sister is working. Until then, want some help arranging and unpacking?"

"Oh. Really. Matt, you've done so much."

"I'm sorry. Let me rephrase. I have to pick up the kids in a couple of hours but until then, DJ and I will help you arrange and unpack."

I kiss her on the cheek a second time, watching her turn a gorgeous shade of pink. She lowers her eyes and shakes her head slightly... Almost like she's trying to figure out if I'm the real deal. I can't say I won't have fun proving to her that, though DJ may joke around with me, and the guys in the department may like calling me on it, not all guys are assholes.

Chapter Five

☆ Mariah ☆

I watch as Matt and DJ work together to start moving furniture and everything into place. I've been banned from lifting a finger, and I'm truly not sure how I feel about that.

"No, that doesn't look right. Go to the left." I'm leaning on the counter next to my laptop. Lyric has requested it be turned into my living room. She's directing the guys on where to put things. Something about... feng shui? She wanted to make sure that my apartment not only looks amazing, but also gives me the most positive feelings. She wanted to make sure I'm making the best of my space, and that it all looks ordered and perfect.

Matt and DJ are following her orders, and I can't say I'm not amused. Two giant guys like them taking orders from a girl half their size.

"How's that?" Matt asks as he and DJ drop the couch where she said to.

"You've gone too far now! A little to the right."

DJ looks at her incredulously before looking back at Matt. "Fuck me...," he mumbles. Matt strips off his shirt, and my eyes widen. I hear

Lyric inhale sharply when DJ follows, throwing his shirt towards my laptop with a glare.

She recovers quickly. "That sounds like fun. Maybe later. Right now, this is so much more satisfying!"

I chuckle as I watch them. "I don't mind the view," I say loud enough for only Lyric to hear me.

"Why does that intense glare DJ just gave me make me wet?"

"Lyric!" I hiss as quietly as possible, hiding my soft laugh behind my hand. I don't think either of us were as quiet as we thought we were because both Matt and DJ's heads snap over to us. We both give them an innocent smile.

"She's like a fucking drill sergeant," Matt says, shooting what looks to me like a smile full of pride.

"I heard that!"

"Then you saw how proud my smile was!"

"Drill Sergeant? Fuck that! She's a brat," DJ says, shooting that same intense glare from earlier at the screen once more.

"I heard that, too!"

"You were meant to. Maybe later I'll watch you spank yourself and imagine it's me."

My eyes widen, and I choke on the water I just took a sip of. "Jesus."

"That sounds like a good time. I'll take a raincheck, though. You have a couch to move." Lyric replies with sass without missing a beat. "Now. Back to the right."

They both lift the couch again, their muscles straining. I can't take my eyes off Matt. The sweat glistening on his arms and back. I want to start setting the barstools up around the counter, but I physically can't tear my eyes away from him.

"Better?" DJ grunts as they put the couch down.

Lyric tilts her head to the side as she thinks. She keeps them hanging for a few moments, trailing her eyes over the couch, before smiling brightly. "It's perfect!"

After a little while of Lyric commanding the room, Matt looks at his watch and sighs. "I have to grab the kids, but when I get back, I'll set them up at the counter with their homework and finish unpacking and setting up your bed."

"Matt..."

"Don't argue. Just be a good girl, and let me help."

I open my mouth to argue, but stop myself and shake my head instead. "Okay. Fine. I'll see you in a little while then?"

"About an hour or so. We'll finish up. I'll buy dinner. And then tomorrow, why don't you come with me to drop the kids off at school? I have them tonight, too. We can go grocery shopping, then get you whatever else you need."

"Is there a point to me disagreeing or arguing with you? Or will you just show up here in the morning and drag me out kicking and screaming?"

He laughs as he walks towards me, throwing on his shirt. He kisses my cheek a third time, and I hate that I'm truly enjoying the feel of his lips against my cheek. "I'll go with option B."

He pushes a strand of my hair behind my ear and turns to leave, leaving DJ on his own to deal with Lyric and her demands and sass.

I have absolutely no fucking clue what I did to deserve a man like him. But I intend to take full advantage of the blessing. The more time I spend with him, the more I like him. And the more I realize that he's nothing like any man I was with before. Nothing like my father. They don't hold a candle to him.

★★★

I will never be used to the Florida heat. I grew up in the North. Where there's snow. And four seasons. Usually all in one day.

"How do you stand this?"

"Stand what?" Matt asks.

"The heat? How do you walk around in full uniform, full equipment and everything, and not die in this heat?"

Matt laughs. We're hauling groceries from his truck into my apartment. I'm fairly convinced I'm going to combust.

He looks me up and down. I can't miss the look of both longing and appreciation in his eyes. I smile shyly and look down, away from him. No one has ever looked at me like that before. Ever. Especially when all I am wearing is jean cutoffs and a t-shirt. The jean cutoffs are pretty short.

Enough that if I bend, they will show my ass. I have large tits, too. Everything I wear looks revealing as fuck. Even when I try to hide them, they are still there. Even still. No one has ever looked at me the way he is right now.

He looks away and holds the door open for me. "Usually, I'm in an air conditioned car."

I smile up at him as we step into the elevator. He hits the button for the top floor. I try not to stare at him, but it's hard. Matt Chance is truly gorgeous, and I absolutely hate myself for noticing. I can't work on my own issues if all I can think about is him and how good he looks in those shorts and that t-shirt. The red Captain America t-shirt stretches across his body like it's painted on him.

I chuckle. "Hmm... So Captain America does have a weakness. Must have air conditioning."

He laughs and winks at me, then gently nudges me. "It'll be our secret."

A few minutes later, after all of the groceries are inside, Matt holds out his hand. "Keys."

I look up at him and crease my eyebrows together. "Why?"

"Because I still have to bring your TV up here. And that bookshelf that I need to put together. Or have you forgotten already?"

I had actually forgotten, but I smile and hand him my keys. He'd already made me agree to let him deal with carrying that stuff up here because it was so heavy. I learned rather quickly that arguing with him is completely pointless. He argues using logic. And arguing against logic isn't possible. At least it's not possible with him.

He leans down and kisses me on the corner of my mouth, and I catch my breath as I close my eyes for a moment. "You are completely unnerving."

"Then I'm making progress because yesterday I was impossible."

I smile and shake my head as I push him towards the door. I fail, though. He's made of pure muscle. It's like trying to move a brick wall. He grabs my wrists and holds them together while he kisses both of them.

"You're still impossible."

"Determined." He kisses the other side of my mouth before he lets me go and walks out the door.

41

Last night was the most fun I'd had in a long time. Maybe ever. After we got all of the stuff arranged and unpacked and put together, Matt took me and the kids to his apartment to order the pizza I'd missed for dinner the night before. DJ stayed back in my apartment. I didn't miss the fiery look that had taken over his entire demeanor. I didn't dare make any attempt to stop him or ask what he was doing. I already had an idea, and I think Matt did, too.

Neither of us mentioned it, though. And when DJ showed up at Matt's apartment about an hour later looking far more like the fun-loving guy I'd met, my suspicions were confirmed. At least to myself. I planned to ask Lyric about it today when I talked to her. I was far too exhausted last night to say anything more than goodnight.

I smile to myself. Matt is a force of nature. It's like he can read me better than even I can. Like he knows I'm trying to push him away, but refuses to let me do it. I've never met anyone like him. I've never met anyone who cared enough about me right away to not let me push him away. It's like he sees the walls I've built and immediately knows where the weakness is. Instead of picking slowly away at it, he crashes right through my weakest point, buries me under the wall, and then pulls me out from under the rubble.

He's ruined me. Sergeant Matt Chance has completely ruined me.

What the hell am I even doing? I left Minnesota to start over. To follow my dreams. To live my life on my own terms. My ultimate dream is to become a successful writer. No one in my family thought I could do it. Not even my now ex. I have one person in my corner. And she doesn't even live in the same country.

I should've moved to the United Kingdom. Somewhere near her and where Matt isn't. I can't allow him to get through my walls. I built them to keep people out. I need to keep people out.

I take a deep breath and take out my phone.

Lyric.

I haven't talked to Lyric since yesterday. She'll help me get through this. I know she will. She always knows what to do.

Mariah: Hey. Do you have a minute?

I look up as Matt unlocks my door and comes in with the TV and the bookshelf. I widen my eyes. "Did you seriously bring them both up together?"

42

"Captain America. Remember?" He winks at me and immediately gets to work.

"Need any help?"

"Nope, I got this." He nods to my phone as it beeps. "Looks like you're in the middle of something anyway."

I look down at my phone. I need her right now. She's the one who got me this far. She'll know what to do.

Lyric: Of course! I always have time for you. Are you doing better today? You must have been exhausted after yesterday.

Mariah: Better every day. Listen, I need your help. With Matt...

Lyric: You already know what I'm going to say.

I sigh because she's right. I know exactly what she's going to say.

Mariah: You're going to tell me that I need to stop fighting it, and let it happen.

Lyric: You know you can't fight it. You're a romantic at heart, and I don't care what you say. I've talked to him twice. I can already tell the guy is perfect for you.

Mariah: This is not at all what I moved here for. I wanted to start over.

Lyric: And just how in the hell does ignoring your feelings and closing yourself off from love help you do that? You're a romance writer, Mariah. And you write romance for a reason. You're a romantic at heart. You couldn't close yourself off from love if you tried.

Mariah: This is so hard to do alone, though...

Lyric: You aren't alone. You never have been alone. You'll always have me. And if yesterday was anything to go by, you now have DJ, too.

I sigh again and chew the inside of my cheek. As right as she is, having someone I can always count on a hug from when I'm freaking out about how ridiculous it is to fall in love with a guy after two stupid days is always nice. I'm not totally sure I'm there with DJ yet, though the fact that I feel like I can trust him, and that he can be that person just as much as Lyric is is strangely comforting.

Lyric: Mariah, you have always had good instincts. When you met the douchedick, you didn't listen to those instincts. You

43

didn't recognize them for what they were. As much as I hate what you went through, you have learned from it. You know better now. And I don't doubt for one second that those instincts are telling you everything you need to know. Trust them. I know it's hard. Hell, I know that's ironic coming from me. You know my past. You know I barely trust anyone. But I also know that you can't cut yourself off from love. You can't deny yourself a life with the love of a man who so clearly adores you. We both know you would never let me do that. So what makes you think I'm going to let you?

Mariah: Actually… Have you thought any more about moving over here? I know you've always dreamed of moving to America.

Lyric: Nice subject change.

Mariah: I'm only leading up to the subject change.

Lyric: Okay… I've been thinking about it a lot recently. And after last night, well, that may be sooner than we think.

I bite my lip and smile as I look up at Matt. His muscles are rippling underneath his t-shirt as he puts the bookshelf together with practiced ease. I smile and giggle because I'm about to finally get that confirmation I want. She's right. I'm a total romantic. I may question myself, but I don't question her and DJ's immediate reaction to each other.

"You okay, beautiful?"

I smile. Beautiful. No one's ever called me beautiful before.

"Yeah. Yeah. I'm okay."

He shoots me his ridiculously sexy, killer smile, and I feel my resolve weakening. He's attaching my bookshelf to the wall. Why does he have to look so good doing it? Hell, why does he have to be who is? Sweet on one hand. Commanding on the other. Sexy on one hand. Protective on the other. I shake my head and look back down at my conversation.

Mariah: So… about DJ.

Lyric: Oh, here we go. I'm totally rolling my eyes.

Mariah: And biting your lip at the thought of him shirtless and sweaty.

Lyric: … No comment.

Mariah: Yeah, that's not working. What happened last night?

44

It takes her a few minutes to answer. I distract myself by watching Matt until my phone dings.

Lyric: He... may... have... um... made me bend over my bed and... spank myself... And oh my God, it was so... so... hot. He... um... He made me move the laptop so he had the perfect view. He could see how much I was enjoying it. I started to tease him a little.

Mariah: Oh my God! Tell me everything!

Lyric: So... he may or may not have asked me if I was as turned on as him. And I... totally said yes. I teased him by sliding my hand into my sexy little shorts, and ran my fingers from my clit to my pussy. I pulled them out of my shorts and held them up so he could see them glistening. I took my teasing further when I slowly licked them before sucking myself off of them... With a very dirty moan.

Mariah: Lyric!

Lyric: DJ, I think, had enough teasing, though, because he completely took command. He nearly yelled my name, but not like he was mad or anything. It was a command. I stopped immediately and looked at the camera. Then he started commanding me to do... stuff.

Mariah: No. You have to tell me.

Lyric: I'm pretty sure you're going to be finding that out on your own. You don't need me to tell you.

My eyes widen as I realize what she's inferring. I look up at Matt again and instantly feel a tingling sensation between my legs I've never felt before him. I shake my head.

Mariah: You do know I'm not letting this go. Matt is busy right now, putting things together. Including a dresser in my bedroom. You need to tell me.

Lyric: Fine... But don't get mad at me when you come without touching yourself.

I chuckle and shake my head. I've never come before. Doubtful I'll be doing it just by reading what happened.

Mariah: Promise. Now spill it.

Lyric: He told me to take off my shirt. I think he expected a bra, but I don't wear bras... His eyes nearly bulged out of his

45

head, and he swallowed hard. He told me to touch my tits. So… I did. He told me to pinch my nipples and play with them. I did. He told me to slowly run my hands down my body and slowly slide my shorts off. I don't know why I kept listening to him. I've never done anything like that before. It was like not only did I not have a choice, but I wanted to do everything he commanded me to do. It felt… natural.

I cross my legs as the tingling feeling gets stronger. Why it's happening, I don't really understand, but some hidden, dark part of me wants her to continue. My breath hitches, and I lick my lower lip, imagining it's Matt doing all of those things to me.

Mariah: What did he tell you to do next?

Lyric: He told me to sit on the bed. To lean back against the wall behind it. To prop a couple pillows behind me and place the laptop down in front of me. He… He told me to spread my legs so he could see what I was doing. I could see him touching himself. He'd unbuttoned his pants. Oh God, Mariah. He's… the biggest I've ever seen. I couldn't stop myself from licking my lips.

I close my eyes and rub my thighs together before opening them to continue reading. The pressure building is becoming intense and not something I'm at all used to. I glance into the bedroom at Matt, making sure he's still busy and not paying attention to me. I'm sure my face has turned hot and red by this point as I think of him touching himself as he watches me.

Lyric: He… told me to tease myself. I was a little unsure. I fumbled around a little, but he told me exactly where to touch and what to do. He told me to stop when I got to my clit and watched me as I teased it. He told me to pinch and rub it. He told me to flick and tug it. I closed my eyes at one point, and he told me to open them and watch him. I couldn't take my eyes off him. He was stroking himself so hard I just wanted him in my mouth. I wanted to lick and suck him.

"Oh, fuck…," I whisper. Just reading this is making me wetter than I ever believed possible. I think of Matt stroking himself, and the tingling is becoming so intense that I'm starting to shake and tremble. I rub my thighs together more to try and relieve the pressure.

Lyric: And then he told me to slide a finger inside myself. I've never done that before. Ever. But I wanted to so badly because the pressure he was making me build in myself was so intense. I felt so dirty and like such a bad girl, but I wanted to make him happy. I wanted to please him. It felt so good. I didn't want to stop.

My eyes widen as my own pressure intensifies. I squeeze my thighs together and suppress a breathless moan while I think of Matt watching me finger myself.

Lyric: I was watching him stroke himself and he got larger and harder. I was fixated on him and his commands. He told me to add another finger and thrust faster and harder. So I obeyed him. I told him I... thought I was going to come. He said he was, too. He told me to keep going. He wasn't there yet. I was trying to hold back. I almost came watching him jerk his dick. He commanded me to come, and we both came so hard. I almost launched off the bed. I screamed his name and came a second time when he screamed mine.

I bite my lip. The pressure intensifies to a level I've never experienced imagining Matt coming as he watches me. I come. I put my hand over my mouth to muffle my moan as my eyes widen. I look over at the bedroom to Matt, hoping he's still busy. It looks like he's finishing the dresser.

Lyric: I fell limp against the pillows. I was trembling, my pussy was clenching and pulsing, as I looked at him through my lashes. And I can honestly say... I have NEVER come as hard as he made me yesterday.

Mariah: What are you going to do? I mean... now... I'm sorry. I may or may not have just come.

Lyric: What? You did not!

Mariah: Uh... yeah. First time for everything. Now. What are you going to do? You've obviously got some kind of strong connection with DJ. You can't just let that slip through your fingers.

Lyric: DJ is... He's amazing. I've only spent a small amount of time with him, and I know there is something there. I have no intention of letting him go. He's the first man I have felt

47

anything for in years. I owe it to myself to at least try. I have all of my paperwork. I'm going to fill it out and buy a ticket. I should be there within the next couple of months or so.

I smile, relieved… in more than one way, then look up and sigh as Matt's grunt and curse bring me slamming back into reality.

Mariah: I'm really happy for you. He seems like everything you've ever wanted. And judging from his reaction to you from what I actually did see, I think he feels the same way…
Lyric: You are probably right. You usually are about these things. Now that I've completely corrupted your innocent mind. Back to Matt. What are you so afraid of?
Mariah: I don't know. He keeps asking me what happened to cause an attack like that. I haven't told him everything...
Lyric: You have to, Mariah. He didn't hesitate to hold you all night long, and he doesn't even know you. He deserves an explanation.

I smile and look up at Matt again as he comes out of the bedroom picking up the mess from the boxes.

Mariah: You're right. He deserves it. I'm going to talk to him right now. Before I lose my nerve.
Lyric: You know I'm here whenever you need me!

I put my phone down as Matt heads for the door with the boxes. "Wait. Matt, um..." He looks at me, and I look down. I take a deep breath. I have to do this. I have to. I look back up at him. "Can we talk?"

"Sure. I was just going to bring these downstairs real quick."

I nod. "Okay…" I bite my lip as I try to hold his gaze.

He nods. "I'll just be a second."

I smile softly as he walks out the door with the boxes. Feeling how wet I am, I dart into the bathroom to quickly clean up and change. I'm already embarrassed I came like that without touching myself. I didn't really think it was possible, and there is no way I'm letting Matt get any inclination that it happened.

Matt comes back just as I'm coming out of the bathroom. Without a word, he holds out his hand for mine. I take another deep breath and take it.

This is it. This is the moment that I find out if Matt is who he comes off as, or if he's just another jerk who has the power to shatter me.

48

It's crazy to feel this way. It's only been two days. But it's true. I haven't felt anything but sadness, emptiness, weakness, and fear for so many years. Matt has managed to make me feel like maybe I deserve more than what I had. He's made me feel happy for the first time in longer than I can remember. He's made me feel hope.

It's because I feel hope, because I trust him so much in such a short time, that he has the power to destroy me. He leads me to my new couch and pulls me down next to him. I don't let go of his hand. I can't. I need him to anchor me, but I'm so afraid he'll be the reason I drown.

Chapter Six

☆ Matt ☆

Finally.

She's finally going to fully open up to me. I can tell by her hand shaking in mine that whatever she's about to say is hard for her.

I sit down on her couch and pull her down next to me. Her grip on my hand is nearly as tight as it was when she showed up on my doorstep more scared than anyone I've ever seen. And I've seen a whole hell of a lot of scared in my eighteen years on the force.

I lean back on the couch, gently pulling her back with me. She looks around her apartment for a few minutes gathering her thoughts.

I bring her hand up to my lips and kiss her knuckles before I let go of it and take it in my other one so I can put an arm around her. As soon as I pull her into my side and hold her close to me, she relaxes. I fucking love that I have the ability to do that.

She rests her head on my shoulder and relaxes her hand that I'm holding in my lap.

"When I was a kid, something like six, I think, one of my dad's friends molested me," she blurts. I inadvertently inhale sharply and squeeze her hand a little too tightly. What the fuck? If I ever find out who this person was, I will use him for target practice. "I'm sorry," she says softly.

"What? For what? Being molested isn't your fault."

"For blurting it out like that. In order for you to understand what put me in the state I was in the other night, I have to start from the beginning." She squeezes my hand softly. I force myself to relax. She needs me to be calm. Not go into protective boyfriend mode. She takes another deep breath. "I told pretty much right away. It only happened once. He was arrested."

"Fucking good."

She burrows into my side a little closer. I hug her tighter. "When I was seven, my dad allowed my stepmother's brother to live with us. He didn't have anywhere to go. He was a senior in high school and was kicked out of the house. I never really knew why. But my dad has a kind heart. He couldn't stand to see him on the street."

She pauses a moment and buries her head in my chest. "It was fine for a while. He babysat when my parents went out. My dad had a band and they had shows. So he stayed with me. Played games. Dolls. Whatever my heart desired. He didn't let anyone mess with me at school. It was a small school. All the grades were under the same roof. Different sections, but the same roof."

I already know where this is going, and I hate it. Another person to use for target practice.

"One day he... started touching me. He told me not to tell or he'd hurt my dad. So... I didn't tell. And it got worse and worse. He'd make me lay with him on the couch under a blanket with my dad and others in the room. I'd plead with my eyes for someone to help, but they never did. Never noticed. I'll never forget that it lasted six months. Until one day... my stepmother walked out and saw. She went to tell my dad. He fled."

She doesn't cry, but she's shaking. I let go of her hand and pull her into my lap. I don't care if it's too soon. I need her there. And I know she needs to be there whether she admits it or not.

I pull her close to me again, and she lays her head on my chest. "I'm so sorry, baby."

She shakes her head. "Don't. Don't be. It made me into the person I am. Minus the panic and anxiety, which didn't come from those

51

experiences. At least, I don't think they did. I'm a strong and fiercely independent woman in large part to that."

"You're the strongest fucking woman I know to get through that and still be standing. To have gotten as far as you have in life."

She's quiet for a full minute before she starts speaking again. "I went through therapy for a little while, but it really didn't help. When it all comes down to it, I got through it on my own. In my own way. And it was those experiences and getting through them that allowed me to make it through everything else. Because I knew if I got through that, I could get through anything."

"I'm so proud of you." My heart constricts in my chest, but I stay strong and steady for her.

"The older I got, the more my dad started falling apart. He's bi-polar paranoid delusional. And maybe schizophrenic. But we didn't know that then. My stepmother seemed to not be capable of thinking more intelligently than a sixteen-year-old. So, the child they had together basically became my responsibility. It was almost like I was a mother at twelve years old."

"Fucking Christ."

"My dad. I mentioned he kept getting worse. He pulled me out of school my freshman year because of a bomb threat. He let me go back the next year, and I was able to make everything up. I worked my ass off. I still would've graduated with my class in two thousand. But then he did it again. He pulled me out my junior year. He used the Columbine massacre as his excuse. Said it was going to happen at my school on Hitler's birthday."

"That was a pretty scary time, though. All schools were on high alert."

"It was. But instead of being logical about it and just keeping me home from school that day, or even that week, he pulled me out completely. He gave me the opportunity to go back again. But it was to another school, and I would've graduated a year later. I was pissed off so I refused. By that time, he had moved us to a small town of four hundred and six people. And actually we were three miles outside of town living in a school bus with a fairly large addition attached to it."

"I can't imagine that was up to code."

"It definitely was not."

52

She shifts and grabs my wrist to look at my watch. I can't help that my cock immediately hardens. I hope she doesn't feel it. "Still a few hours before the kids are done, Rih."

"I like them."

I grin and kiss her cheek. I really love that she likes my sister's kids. My family is my entire world. "Yeah, they grew on me a little bit."

She smiles back, and then puts her head back on my shoulder. "We lived in an area with no trees. Nothing to really stop the wind. And the wind got bad. I hated it. My room was always cold. And then one day, a tornado hit. It went right over our... whatever it was we were living it. I called it a shack. Didn't touch down until it was two miles away and over water, but when it passed over, it shook everything. It was almost like an earthquake, except you could feel it sucking you up instead of swallowing you into the ground. We had no basement. No shelter. That's when the panic started. Really started. It had always been there. At least a little. Mild but it was there."

"I can't really say I blame you."

"It was really lonely, too. I didn't have any friends. All I had was my dad and stepmother and little brother. Ten years younger. So nothing in common. I didn't care to listen to my dad's conspiracy theories. And my stepmother watched TV all day. I had two friends. One was seventy-six miles away. The other was down the road, but I obviously couldn't spend all day with her, and she was in school most of it anyway. Honestly, it was the being alone that got me. Too much time to think. Thinking made me freak out about everything. The future. My life."

She rests her hand on my stomach, and I close my eyes. I force myself to breathe deeply, but it helps me none. Her hair. I've smelled coconut before, but on her... God, she smells amazing. I give in and breathe her in as I tighten my grip around her.

"Right before I turned eighteen, I had made plans to move. I didn't want to live with my dad anymore. I was born in Minnesota, but part of my dad's paranoia led to a move to Montana when I was nine. My plan was to move back to Minnesota with my mom and grandmother. My whole family, really. Anyway, one day I was walking home from that one friend's house, and I fell in a gopher hole or snake or something. I twisted my ankle really bad, but I limped my way home. I was late, but not by much."

She grips my shirt in her hand, and I twist my fingers in her hair.

"My dad was pissed. He accused me of lying. He slapped me really hard. I remember my chest getting really tight. I couldn't breathe. He slapped me a second time because I didn't answer him when he said something to me. Next thing I know, I woke up in the hospital with the Sheriff and a friend of my dad's next to me. I lost five days of my life. I'd had a really bad panic attack and passed out. I had gone in and out of consciousness for the entire day."

"And your dad wasn't even there?"

"Nope. His friend was closer to my age anyway. He only stuck around as long as he had for my sake. And the Sheriff knew everything that was going on. My dad's conspiracy theories were getting so much worse. So he helped me out. He forced the hospital to keep me until I turned eighteen. And then he took me in until my mom was able to get me. He went and got all of my belongings for me and had them shipped to my mom's.

"Holy shit, honey. I don't even know what to say right now."

"I don't have to continue if you don't want me to." She says it so quietly that it breaks my heart.

"Why would I not want you to?"

"Because it's a lot. You're learning my entire life story, and you've only known me three days."

"I told you I wanted to know what happened to make you so scared the other day, baby. I meant it. I want to know. And if this is how you need to do it, I'm listening."

"I thought you would've run by now."

"I'm a cop. I don't run away."

She hugs me. "Thank you. For staying."

I tug her hair so she's looking at me. "I'm not going anywhere."

She smiles softly. "After I moved, I went back to school. Graduated. Put myself through college. By the time I met my ex and got married, the attacks were non-existent. I thought I beat it. Things were great for a while. Then, they started to fall apart." She shrugs and curls back up on me.

I hug her even tighter, sensing she needs it. There's nothing else in the world I want more than this right now. Her. In my arms. No matter the reason or the way she ended up here, all I want is her.

54

"I told you some stuff about him… I didn't say everything." She pauses and takes a deep breath. "At first I didn't care. He had health issues. Mental as well as physical. But then about six years ago, he really changed. He didn't seem attracted to me anymore. Didn't want to touch me. Told me my hair is gross, or that I smelled… um... down... there. I don't. I'm a very clean person, but that's what he started saying. He'd insult me like that all the time. He'd tell me I'm fat. He'd call me names. Like bitch and stuff. And then he'd say that he was joking. And then he started getting sick all the time."

"Whoa. Hang on. He went from being a good guy to calling you names and not wanting to touch you?"

"When I really think about it and be honest, he'd always been like that. But it got worse. He'd never really made me feel pretty or wanted. And it always ended up being about him. Eventually, with his health issues and things, I put my entire life on hold for him. I stopped writing. I stopped talking to people. Eventually, it was like Montana again. I had no one. I lost myself."

She looks up at me, and I see the fire in her eyes. I can't help but feel pride at just how strong this girl is. How far she's come.

"Last year, he had a health crisis that ended with surgery. I dropped everything. I used all of my personal time off. I went on a leave of absence to be with him in the hospital. I thought that was it. That's why everything fell apart. Because he wasn't feeling well. I thought it would fix it. I took care of him. I sacrificed everything to make sure he was okay. But after it was all said and done, nothing changed. Nothing at all. Everything was still the same."

She glares at the wall.

"Finally, I had had enough. I couldn't take it anymore. I decided I needed to get myself back. By that time, I was getting the anxiety back. Walking into a store would send me into a panic attack. Walking out of the house would send me into a panic attack. I hated it. So, I started writing again. I put my stuff on this app that I found. People loved my stuff. I started to get my confidence back. I met Lyric through my writing. She helped me see that I could reach all my writing goals; all my personal goals. She gave me the confidence to publish. She was with me every step of the way. And she helped me see that I needed better for myself. We became fast friends and got each other through a lot." She looks up at me.

"I wouldn't be here without her. Everyone else gave up on me. Didn't believe in me or show any support for me. She's all I have."

"Not anymore, Rih. You have me. I'm not going anywhere. You have DJ, too. And remind me to thank her for bringing you into my life."

"Even though I'm certifiably crazy?"

I reach up and touch her cheek. She leans into my hand. "You are definitely not crazy."

"Are you sure? We haven't gotten to the part where I freaked out and crawled into bed with a man I just met."

I can't help but chuckle and pull her back into me. "The change got to you. Everything changing and you not being able to process everything at once. I bet you felt like you couldn't handle it. Couldn't do it. Like you made a mistake. Apart from Lyric, you were alone. And while she helped, it wasn't enough. You didn't have anyone there with you. Not physically anyway. I'm just glad I was there, that she convinced you to come to me, and that you trusted me enough to let me help you."

"That's... exactly how I felt. And I'm glad I trusted you, too."

"You have me. You have DJ. You have your friend, Lyric. I'm not going anywhere, DJ isn't going anywhere, and I don't think Lyric is either."

It's like an entire hundred pound weight has been lifted. The tension she was holding onto releases, and she sinks completely into me. "You don't know how happy I am to hear that."

I look at my watch. "We have to go. Grab some stuff for the night. You're staying with me."

She looks up at me, the most adorable bewildered look on her face. "What? Why?"

I can't help it. I kiss the corner of her mouth. "Because after everything you just shared, I want you close to me in case you end up in another attack. I'm sure that was mentally exhausting."

"Well, yeah, but-"

"Nope. You're staying with me. No argument. Now, go."

She slowly climbs out of my lap, trying to think of something to say and failing. When she's standing, I smile and swat her ass.

"Hey!"

I grin. "That's for arguing so much with me. Now go."

She stares in open-mouthed shock for a second before she disappears in her room.

I had already made up my mind about her, but her sharing all of that sealed the deal for me. Her trust in me after all that is astounding. I won't break it. From now on, I will absolutely be her fiercest protector. She'll never be alone or fight alone again as long as I'm breathing.

Chapter Seven

☆ Mariah ☆

(One Week Later)

I slowly and sleepily open my eyes, but I don't know what woke me up. I blink, then burrow back into my bed. Moments later, I hear what sounds like knocking. "What the hell?"

I get out of bed and walk cautiously to the door.

"Rih? Please wake up."

"Matt?"

He knocks again, and I unlock the door, opening it only a crack. Standing on the other side is a frantic-looking Matt half dressed in his uniform. It's almost a week after we talked. We've spent every day together since, but I'm confused because he's supposed to be starting his days off today.

"Thank God. Fuck, thank God. I need your help."

I look at him, half asleep and fully confused. "What's wrong? Are you drunk?"

He smiles and laughs. "No. Nothing like that. I got a callout for SWAT. My parents are out of town this weekend, and I have my sister's kids. She's working. I can't leave them alone because I don't know how long I'll be gone. This call is big. We have our team and almost everyone working tonight on patrol out there. I need you to stay with the kids. Please, Rih."

"Yeah. Yeah, of course I will. You don't even have to ask." I rub my eyes and yawn. "Let me just get my laptop, so I can work."

I turn for my laptop. Matt holds the door, waiting for me. I hurry and grab my keys on the way out, following him to his apartment, and to his bedroom.

"You can sleep in my room. The kids get woken up at seven. My sister keeps them on a schedule. Whatever they want for breakfast is fine." He walks to his closet and pulls out a large gym bag. "If you need anything, just text. I'll try to answer."

I follow him back out to the living room. "Matt, I got this. We'll be fine."

He turns to me and grins. He slips an arm around me and leans down to kiss me. I expect the cheek, head, or the corner of my mouth because that's all he's ever kissed before, but his lips meet mine, and my entire body feels like it explodes into a firework show.

I reach out and grab his arm to steady myself as his kiss becomes a little harder. It's like my entire world has flipped upside down. I've never felt like this before. I've never felt like my entire world just falls away, and all that's left is me and him. His touch. His scent. His lips.

"Uncle Matt? Do you have to go to work?"

Matt pulls back slowly and kneels down in front of his six-year-old niece. "Yeah, sweetheart. I got a call and there's some people who need help." Marie hugs him tightly and Brit comes out to join in. His twelve year old nephew, Beckett, sleepy comes out of his room as well. He hugs them all and kisses them each on the forehead before he stands again. "Mariah's going to stay with you, so be good. She'll tell me everything. Now go back to bed."

They each hug him again, then scurry back to their rooms. Matt slips an arm around me once more. He leans down and gives me a quick kiss, then taps my ass.

"I think you have an obsession with my ass."

59

"I definitely have an obsession with your ass. Probably a little with your tits, too." He kisses me quickly again before I have a chance to respond. "I gotta go. Thank you."

Matt kisses me again and hurries out of the apartment. I poke my head into the kid's rooms. Brit and Marie are curled up in their beds. Beckett is curled up in his room. They are all already tucked back in and sleeping peacefully. I leave the door open a crack and walk to Matt's room. I don't expect to get any sleep, so I set an alarm on my phone and open my laptop, pulling up my new book.

Before I know it, I've written a ton, and my alarm is going off. "Shit. Seven already."

I quickly save my work and get up to wake up the kids. I had been on a roll, and I'm really excited to get this next book done.

"Kids? Time to get up."

They don't move so I enter the room and shake them awake. After they seem to be moving, I head to Beckett's room.

"Beckett? Time to wake up."

"Uncle Matt?" Beckett asks sleepily.

"Still working, sweetheart. But I thought we could make breakfast together. How do you guys feel about breakfast quesadillas?"

"What's that?" Marie asks, coming up behind me.

"Oh, gosh. You are in for a treat. You can put anything in them!"

While they finish their morning routine, I find one of Matt's hoodies. I'm a little chilled. Once we're all finished, we all head to the kitchen.

"Okay. So first things first. We need eggs." I open the fridge and start pulling out ingredients. "We need some cheese. And sour cream. Some bacon and sausage. We need some shells. I'm so happy all this stuff is here." I put everything on the counter and arrange it neatly. "Ready?"

"What do we do?" Beckett asks.

"First, we have to start the bacon and sausage. And while we're doing that, you girls get to scramble the eggs and set up the rest of the ingredients. Have you done that before? Cracked eggs in a bowl and mixed them up?"

"Yep! We make pancakes with Uncle Matt all the time," Marie says.

"They are really good!" Brit contributes.

60

"Yummy! I bet they are," I say with a smile.

"Sometimes we put chocolate chips in them," Brit says

"And I like bananas," Marie says

"Oh! And cream on top!" Brit says as she jumps up and down.

The girls continue chattering excitedly as Beckett helps me get the rest of the ingredients together. Just as we're putting everything together and starting to cook the quesadillas, Matt walks in looking tired as can be. He hides it as the two girls rush to him.

"Matt!" Marie shrieks.

"Uncle Matt! You're home!" Brit yells.

"Hey, rugrats." He kneels to hug them. They both squeal as he lifts each of them with one arm. God, he's so strong. So sexy. "I missed you."

They both kiss him on the cheek, and he puts them down. He ruffles Beckett's hair. Beckett laughs. He then walks to me and slips both arms around my waist, pulling my back to his chest. He bends to kiss my neck and shoulder.

"And I missed you. You look incredible in my hoodie."

I look up at him and smile. "Really? You missed me?"

"Yeah. Really. I did miss you. And you really do look incredible in my clothes."

He lets go of me, but runs his hand down my ass, keeping what he's doing blocked from the kids' view. I inadvertently let out a whimper as he gives it a light squeeze. Straightening up, he lets me go and takes a step back. I glare at him.

He smirks. "Smells delicious in here," he says huskily.

"I hope you don't mind that I hijacked your kitchen. We decided on quesadillas."

I finish plating them and cutting them. Matt sits next to the kids as I put the plate in front of them. "We have egg and cheese. We have sausage, egg, and cheese. And we have bacon, egg, and cheese."

"Wow." He looks at them hungrily, and I grin.

"We helped!" Brit exclaims.

"We helped with the eggs. Beckett and Mariah cooked, and we all put them all together!" Marie says.

"They did very well. The eggs are the best tasting eggs I've ever had, and the bacon and sausage is perfect." I wink at the kids.

Matt laughs. "I can't wait to taste them."

We all dig in. We talk and laugh. We goof off. It all seems so incredibly normal. So right.

And it scares me to death. I try not to let my fear show, but I do get quieter.

After a little while, Matt is in full Lego building mode with Marie, Brit, and Beckett. I take it as my cue to head out. I sneak back to his room and remove his hoodie, then grab my laptop and phone. I turn to leave and see Matt leaning against the doorway.

He smiles. "Trying to sneak out on me?"

"I didn't want to get in the middle of your family time." I say the words quietly. "And I stayed up all night writing. So I'm kind of tired. I was going to take a nap."

He smiles a little more and crooks his finger at me, beckoning me to him. I put my laptop and phone on the bed and do as I'm told. He puts his arms around me and pulls me close to him. With one hand, he pushes my hair behind my ear, then pulls my hair so my head is tilted up. His lips meet mine in a heated and hot kiss. A kiss that takes my breath away while at the same time breathing life into me.

It doesn't take long for Matt's hand at the small of my back to find its way to my ass. He backs me into his room and turns me so that I'm pressed against the wall. My hands move from his chest to his back. I pull him closer until he's pressed against me so hard that I don't know where I begin and he ends. I want him. I've never actually wanted anyone like this before. I need him. I need him like I need air. Maybe more.

His tongue finds mine, and we both moan.

Oh... God.

The taste of him. It's like it consumes me. I can't get enough. Like if I don't taste him, I'll die.

"Uncle Matt!" Brit yells.

I quickly pull away and push him back slightly. He tightens his grip around me. "What do you need, Brit?"

"We don't know where this piece goes!"

I smile up at him as he presses his hips into me. I gasp at the feel of his hard cock against me. He grins. My body has a complete mind of its own, and I press myself against him.

"Uncle Matt!" Brit yells again.

"Give me a minute, you guys." His eyes don't leave mine. Reflected in them is my own desire. Need.

"Cockblocked," I tease.

"By my sister's fucking kids."

I reach up and run my hand over his cheek. I've grown to love his stubble. He leans down to kiss me again.

"Matt!" Marie yells.

Matt groans as he pulls me away from the wall. "I'll call you for dinner later."

"You don't have to -" He spanks me. Hard. "Ow! Matt, what the hell?" I try to keep my voice low so the kids don't hear me as my hands fly to my ass.

He leans down close to my ear, his hand firmly squeezing my ass. "Keep arguing." He rubs my ass cheek where the sting from his hand lingers. "I'm enjoying it, beautiful."

His breath is hot against my ear, and his large hand rubbing the sting away gives me butterflies I've never felt for anyone but him. A heat begins between my legs that I've also never felt for anyone but him. He kisses me softly.

"Oh my God..."

"Like I was saying. Dinner. I'm not letting you do your not eating thing."

"I eat."

"Not enough." He lets me go and grabs the hoodie I was wearing. He puts it over my head and helps me back into it.

"What are you doing to me?"

"Not letting you build up the walls I've worked so hard to get through." He kisses me again and then leaves the bedroom.

I walk out of the room and try to quietly sneak past without interrupting Matt and the time he has with the kids. It's so obvious to me that he cherishes that time. His family truly means the world to him.

He turns to me as I quietly walk past him. "Did DJ mention his son's birthday party? It's coming up soon."

I pause. "Um... Yeah. He texted about it. I put it in my calendar. He said I'm supposed to go with you, and if I don't show, he's sending the SWAT team to pick me up."

Matt laughs. Marie squeals and runs towards me. She wraps her arms around my waist and looks up at me with pretty doe eyes. "You're really coming with us?"

I smile and hug her back. "Looks like it, munchkin."

"Yay!" she screams.

"We have a little time," Matt says as he stands up from his place on the floor. "We can plan it out a little. You can help us pick out the birthday presents. I'm in charge of the cake. I planned on an ice cream cake, but I'll have to order it soon to get it reserved."

I look up at him in horror as he reaches me. Marie goes back to their Lego project. "You can't get an ice cream cake. Good Christ. It'll melt before we get to his house. And you aren't buying one."

He laughs. "I don't bake, beautiful."

I shake my head, trying to make the terrifying thoughts of a melted ice cream cake vanish from my mind's eye. I hold up a hand. "I'll make the cake." I shake my head and shiver as I turn away. "Ice cream cake. Fuck me."

He grabs my arm gently and pulls me back to him. He leans down and kisses me gently before whispering in my ear. "Soon."

I shiver again, but for a totally different reason. His deep voice reverberates throughout my entire body.

Holy hell.

Good Christ. This man.

What am I doing here? What is he doing to me?

Whatever it is, it's something that's never happened before, and I can't decide how to feel about it. He scares me. I'm scared to feel. I'm so scared I'll get hurt. And I know I won't be able to come back from it this time.

64

Chapter Eight

☆ Matt ☆

(One Month Later)

I sit down on a chair in the turnout room and glare at the front of the room. It's been a little over a month since I kissed Mariah in my bedroom, and I can feel her pulling further and further away from me as the days go by.

It's not that she doesn't let me kiss her. Or even touch her. She talks to me. Spends time with me. When I have my sister's kids, she spends time with all of us, but she's withdrawn. She's quiet. She looks tired. Sick. And the headaches. She downplays them, but I can tell how much they hurt her.

And eating. The thing that pisses me off the most is she's been throwing herself into writing and literally forgetting to eat. If I didn't make her eat dinner with us, I seriously doubt she'd eat at all.

Her anxiety is almost constant. Another thing she tries to hide. But she can't hide that shit from me. I see it.

The pencil in my hand snaps in half. I found it on the table when I sat down. I'm so pissed off, I hadn't even realized that I picked it up at all.

"Dude. What the fuck is wrong with you?"

I look over at DJ, and shake my head. "Nothing."

"Really? Because the past few days you've been kind of a dick. Yesterday, you wrote a mother of two a ticket for nineteen over because she was trying to get her kid from daycare before they closed."

I shrug. "She shouldn't have been doing nineteen over. Not like she won't be able to get her kid."

"Matt, you know some daycares charge an entire extra day if you're late. You would've let that person go, or at the very least dropped her to ten. Gave her a break on the cost."

I glare at him. He's absolutely right. I have been being an asshole. Not giving breaks where I typically do. I've been snappy with people. "Okay, yeah. I've been being a dick." I take a deep breath and focus ahead. "It's Mariah."

He looks at me incredulously. "You seriously think I didn't know that?"

I chuckle. "Something is going on. I can tell. She's being a little secretive. She's gotten a couple of phone calls that she runs to my room or her room to take, depending on where we are. And when she's through with the call, she's like a scared little girl. She won't tell me what's going on. She isn't eating. Or sleeping. She can be in my arms, DJ. And it's like she's not there at all. But still, she clings to me. Like I'm the only thing holding her together."

We both fall quiet as Captain McKay goes through turnout and gives out assignments. After he's done, DJ and I walk out to our squads.

"So you think something big is going on?"

"I don't know if it's big, but it's something. I think it might have to do with her dad, though."

"Her dad? That would make a lot of sense since he's the cause of her anxiety and panic."

"Yeah. I've heard her say something about her dad in those conversations. Referring to him. I don't know what to make of it."

"Well, it probably has to do with him, but I don't know what. I'll admit she's been a little distant, though. I mean, I know I haven't known her that long, but I like to think we've gotten pretty close."

"All I know is I can't get her to talk to me. And I thought we were over that bullshit."

66

I open the door to my squad and get in, starting my vehicle check. DJ starts to walk towards his but turns back. "Hey, what about Lyric? They tell each other everything."

"They usually message each other on Instagram, though. Or Skype. I don't have an Instagram page. I fucking hate social media. I won't get one of those fucking pages unless I have no other option."

"Matt, I hate to say it, but it looks like we're there. She ain't eating or sleeping. She's shutting down. You either need to set up a page to talk to Lyric or call her yourself. I can talk to her and find out what's going on, but you need to be able to contact her yourself anyway. We need to figure out what happened before you lose Mariah. Before we both do."

I sigh as DJ gets in his squad. I finish my check and head out on patrol. After a few hours of calls and traffic stops, things slow down, and I pull into a parking lot. I texted and called Mariah several times over my shift, and she hadn't answered anything. I haven't had a chance to talk to DJ since we've both been so busy, so I don't know if he contacted Lyric or not. I'm honestly starting to get worried. It's not like Mariah to completely ignore me. I take out my phone and try calling her again. She doesn't answer.

"Fuck. Baby, you're scaring me. Please call me back." I hang up and rub my head as another call comes in. Domestic disturbance. Fuck. I reluctantly head towards the call resigning myself to the fact that I'm going to have to get Lyric's phone number.

I haven't had a social media account in years. Not since my ex plastered naked pictures of me all over her Facebook page and on a website. We had been in a long distance relationship, and after we met and got together, she became jealous of any woman I was seen with. Her revenge for me dancing with one of my friend's wives at their wedding was to plaster the pictures I'd sent to her all over her Facebook page. They ended up on a pornography website, and I nearly lost my job.

I deleted all of my social media pages. I filed a lawsuit against her. I filed a cease and desist order against the website and requested the images be taken down, as they were not put up with my permission. Nothing came of the lawsuit, and I truly didn't care. All I cared about was my job. At least I was able to get the pictures removed. My hope is they never resurface again. And I hope I don't need to resort to opening a fucking Instagram account.

I force my mind to clear as I pull up to the call. A domestic disturbance is one of the most dangerous calls a cop can go on. We get them more often than we'd like to, and we never know what we're walking into. We don't know if things are flying, if someone is being killed, if someone has a weapon. It's very difficult for our dispatch to get information in intense situations.

As soon as my partner pulls up, we both approach the house. There's screaming and yelling coming from inside. Something shatters as I knock. Hard.

"Gainesville Police Department! Open the door!" I yell as authoritatively as I can.

"You called the police? Fucking bitch!" a male voice growls from inside the door. We hear something else crash, and a scream. I look at my partner, and we kick open the door.

"Gainesville Police! Get off her! Now!" I pull the guy off the woman as my partner immediately checks on her.

What seems like hours later, I'm finally able to clear the call, and the thoughts of Mariah slam into me full force. I need to figure out what's going on. I try calling her again. She doesn't answer. I nearly crush my phone in my hand.

"Squad four to twenty-seven," DJ says over the radio, calling me by my squad.

I pick up my mic. "Go ahead."

"Can I call you?"

"Yeah, I'm free." Seconds later my cell phone is ringing. I raise an eyebrow when I see that it's DJ's squad cell phone number. "DJ? Why are you calling my personal cell from your squad cell?" I don't know what it is, but I'm immediately on high alert. DJ would never call me on my personal cell phone from his squad cell phone if we're working. That's what we have squad cellphone's for.

"Because I'm on my personal one with a rather hysterical Lyric."

My eyes widen. "What? Why! She's in the UK!" My heart rate spikes, and my chest heaves. "What's happening? Why is she hysterical?" I ask frantically. No fucking way she'd call if it wasn't an emergency. Her and DJ talk over skype and Instagram and text just like she and Mariah do. She would only ever call if it were an emergency. I don't even need to ask.

68

Everything that's been going on today with not being able to get ahold of Mariah... I know it has to do with her.

"She's calling because she can't calm Mariah down. Mariah is panicking. Something about her dad up in Duluth in a standoff with the cops. The cops have been calling her all fucking day. Lyric said just when she gets her calmed down, they call again."

"What the fuck! Why the hell didn't she call me?"

"Lyric said because she knew you're working. She didn't want to bother you. You know how Mariah is. I'm pulling up now. I came from across town."

I throw on my lights and sirens and whip around doing a U-turn in the middle of the street and racing for home. "Don't you fucking leave her side," I growl as I speed through the streets.

"Don't intend to. Where's the extra key?"

"Damn. I have it. Fuck!"

"If she doesn't answer, I'll bust down the door." There's a pause on the other line. "Shh... Lyric, baby, I'm there. It's okay. I'm going up now. And Matt's on his way."

"DJ... Don't you hang up with me."

"I won't." I hear him continuing to comfort Lyric, forcing himself to be far calmer than I know he feels. Over the past month, he's gotten a lot closer to Mariah than he lets on. He may be just as protective of her as I am. I hear him running up the stairs to her door. Moments later, he's pounding on it. "Mariah? Mariah, answer the door! It's DJ!"

"Fuck!" I pound on the steering wheel and step harder on the gas.

"Mariah! Open the door!"

"Come on, baby," I whisper.

"Mariah!" There's another pause. "Lyric. Honey, calm down. Now. You need to be strong for me so I can get to her."

"Bust down the fucking door, DJ!" I command.

"It's unlocked, Matt. Fuck, you need to calm down, too," His voice is just as dominating as mine would be if I wasn't completely freaking the fuck out. "Mariah! Where are you, sweetheart?"

My arms are shaking with how hard I'm gripping the steering wheel. "Fuck, DJ. Tell me she's okay."

"I haven't found h-" He cuts himself off.

My vision nearly goes black with how panicked I am. "DJ!"

69

"I found her… Mariah? Look at me, sweetheart."

"Fuck. Thank fuck." I dial my Captain's number and wait impatiently for him to answer.

"What's up, Chance?"

"Brody, listen. Mariah's in one fuck of a panic attack. So much so that her friend in the UK called DJ."

"Go. I'll have dispatch make you a call for it. Keep me informed. If you need the rest of the night off, I'll take care of it."

"Thanks, Cap." I swing my car into the parking lot, squealing the tires and coming to a screeching halt.

"Lyric. I got her, baby," DJ says. "She's okay. Breathe for me. You need to breathe for me, baby. Both of you need to breathe for me. Come on. Deep breaths. Right now."

I run into the apartment building and straight for the stairs. Screw waiting for the elevator. I reach Mariah's door and stop to take a deep breath, nearly slamming the door open. "DJ? Mariah? I'm here! Where are you?" I look around her apartment. Her bedroom. Bathroom. Office. "Baby, where are you?"

She's not in here.

Fuck.

Calm down, Matt. Calm the fuck down.

Think. I need to fucking think.

The phone. In my hand. "DJ? Where are you? Where's my girl?"

"Balcony. We're on the balcony."

I look towards her balcony and rush towards it, exploding through the door. Mariah is curled in the corner. She looks up at me and jumps. Her phone is clutched in her hand. Her eyes are red and bloodshot. Tears are streaming down her face. DJ is knelt next to her holding her close.

"They…" Mariah bursts into a fresh wave of tears.

I drop down next to her and pull her into my lap, burying my face in her hair. "I got you baby. I'm here."

"Matt's here, baby. He's got her," DJ says into his phone. "I'm putting you on speaker."

"Baby, I'm here. And Lyric is on the phone. DJ is right next to us. You're not alone, baby." Her body is overcome with sobs, and I hold her as tightly as I can. I run my fingers through her hair and my hand up and down her back.

"We're here, Mariah. I promise it's okay," Lyric says tearfully.

"It's not. It's not okay!" She tries to get up, but my grip on her is too strong. "I have to go to Duluth! He needs me! They're going to kill him!"

I cuddle her into my chest. "Baby, what happened? Tell me what happened." Her heart is racing. "Lyric, she feels like she's going to have a fucking heart attack. Tell me what to do!" I may have just snapped at her, but all I can think of, all I can care about right now, is Mariah.

"Dude, don't fucking yell at her. She's having a hard enough time. How would you feel if Mariah was going through this, and you were six thousand fucking miles away? Give her a break," DJ scolds me. I know he's right.

"DJ, it's okay. He's just worried. We all are," Lyric says quietly.

"Doesn't give him the right to be an asshole," DJ says, glaring at me.

I take a deep breath as I hug Mariah. "No. DJ's right. I'm sorry. I'm sorry, Lyric. Please... Tell me what I need to do. Help me help her."

"The same thing you did when she first met you. She needs to feel you," she says shakily.

I shift her so her head is against my chest and force myself to breathe normally. I hold her close and tightly, rocking back and forth with her. "Baby. Concentrate on me right now. Okay? Focus on my breathing." She turns her head so that she's breathing in my scent. My cologne. "It's just us. Okay? Can you feel me breathing?"

"Yes," she sniffles. DJ rubs a hand up and down her back.

"The five senses," Lyric nearly whispers, choking back her own sobs. "Get her to focus on her senses. Seeing. Hearing. Feeling. She told me once that it calms her if she's focusing on what's around her."

I nod. "Okay, honey. Keep breathing with me. What do you see?"

"Y-you."

"What color is my uniform?"

"D-dark blue."

"Good girl. What do you feel?" I keep my voice as steady as my breathing. Just as calm. I keep running my fingers through her hair as I hold her.

"Your breathing."

"Good girl. What else?"

71

"Your fingers in my hair. Your arms around me. DJ. He's rubbing my back." I kiss the top of her head. "Your gun belt."

"Good girl. Tell me what you hear, beautiful."

"Your voice. Your breathing. Your heartbeat."

"Tell me what you smell."

"Your cologne. Surrounding me."

Her heartbeat begins to slow as I continue my methodical rhythm rubbing her back and her hair.

"Mariah? Are you okay?" Lyric asks, whimpering quietly.

"Better. A little. Still coming down."

"Focus on Matt. Just him. His breathing and his scent. You love how he smells. And how he feels," Lyric says as calming as she can.

I can't help but smile a little into her hair. I know my effect on her, but the fact that she talks about it to Lyric makes me swell with a strange kind of pride.

"Are you okay, baby?" DJ asks, concerned.

"Don't worry about me. I'm okay. It helps knowing she's okay."

"Come on," DJ says. "I know better than that. I can hear it in your voice."

"I just need to know she's okay," she whispers after a small pause.

"Lyric, I'm okay. I'm coming down." Mariah's breathing regulates more and more the longer I hold her and rock with her. Just when I think she's going to be okay, her phone rings, and she stops breathing.

"Fuck," I whisper.

"Is that her phone? Don't let her answer it. She's had enough!" Lyric says, frantically.

I take Mariah's phone out of her hand and answer it. "Hello?"

"Hello. This is Officer Howard of the Duluth Police Department. I'm looking for Mariah Carter."

"Officer Howard. This is Sergeant Chance with the Gainesville Police Department. What the hell is going on up there?"

I can feel Mariah's pulse starting to race as Officer Howard clears his throat. I know I threw him off, and he probably hates that he's talking to a superior officer right now. I look at DJ, still crouched next to us.

"Take Mariah inside. Take your phone with you. Hold her tightly. Get her away from this. Mariah and Lyric are done dealing with this."

DJ nods and stands taking his phone.

72

Mariah clings to me. "No. Please, Matt. Let me stay with you!"

I kiss her. "Baby, let me deal with this. Please go with DJ. You're safe, honey. You're okay. DJ won't let you go. You know that. You trust him." She cries as DJ helps her get up, and being forced to let her go breaks my heart. Her crying kills me. "Start talking, officer." I growl the words into the phone, incredibly angry at his previous disrespectful tone.

"I... uh... I'm not sure how much I should say. I don't know if you really are a Sergeant. This is a private matter."

I glare at the phone, his tone infuriating me, then take a pic, making sure my name tag and stripes are visible. "I sent you a picture. Now tell me what the hell is going on up there."

He pauses. I grow more and more impatient and furious. Through the window, I can see DJ rocking Mariah back and forth as she cries and grips his vest.

"For the past few weeks, Mariah's father has been calling us with crazy shit. Murders he's witnessed. Where the bodies are buried. Cops he knows are in on some giant cover up. The problem is the murders never happened. He tells us where bodies are, but they aren't there. He points out cops who committed these crimes while on the job, but these guys weren't even cops at the time he says the shit happened. Some weren't even born."

"What does any of that have to do with Mariah?"

"Medical history. We've dealt with him a lot, but no one ever entered notes regarding his medical history. Just mental health issues and combativeness with police. No details. Her number is listed as a contact, and I assume it has to do with the fact that she'll just tell us what the history is. I've been entering notes all day, but I'm the only one, and I don't know if it will work anyway. Some of the guys are lazy fuckers, and I doubt they'll look at previous history."

I take a deep breath while keeping an eye on my girl. "I was told you guys are in a standoff with him."

"Yes, sir. He accused the downstairs neighbor of being in on these murders. He's barricaded himself in the apartment until we arrest the neighbor. Which we aren't doing. So he's decided he's going to deal with the problem on his own. He's threatened to kill the neighbor. Says he has a gun. We aren't leaving until he comes out. We're taking him for a fifty-one-fifty. I've been trying to get Mariah to help us out. She did talk to him

73

for nearly two hours for me. It didn't end well, but I thought we could try again."

I force myself to reign in my temper. A fifty-one-fifty is a psych hold. Thank fuck they're at least doing that. "How many times have you called her today?"

"Uh... Well, I've been her contact, sir. I've probably talked to her maybe six or seven times."

"And during any of those calls, officer, did you notice any changes in her? Maybe during that fucking two hour one? Did you think that, perhaps, you were, I don't know, causing undue stress and a fucking panic attack that may very well land her in the hospital?"

"Sir -"

"Did I say you could speak?"

"N-no, sir."

"Then don't. You didn't bother to ask at all about her history with her father. You didn't use any of your training to listen to her. You didn't notice classic panic attack signs. You're too focused on one particular aspect of the situation instead of the entire picture. And now I have a scared out of her mind girl who's fighting to breathe and in the midst of a complete fucking freak out because she's fifteen hundred miles away and can't do anything. You didn't think for a second the effect on her."

I stand up and lean against the railing, still watching Mariah. The officer takes a few discreet deep breaths. I'm positive he suddenly feels like an asshole for doing this to her.

"So, here's what's happening. Take her number out of your system. You don't need to be calling every time you deal with her father. Do what you have to do. Notate it saying to leave her the hell alone. I don't care what you have to do. Make it happen. She doesn't need this shit. If she gets one more phone call, I'm going straight to your Chief. Understand?"

"Yes, sir."

"She only gets a phone call in emergency situations. I don't think I need to explain to you what the fuck that would be. Questions?"

"No, sir."

"Good. Until this is resolved, you call me. You do not call her. I'll text you my number."

"And she only gets a call if there's an emergency."

"You got it."

74

"I'll take care of it."

I sigh. "How is he? What's going on?"

"Our Tactical Response Team is planning to enter. They're giving him one more chance, but he says if they come in, they'll die."

I rub my temple. "Fuck."

"I thought she might be able to talk him down, but I for sure needed to know if she knew what kind of weapons he has."

"She doesn't. She hasn't been in Duluth for over a month. Lot of shit could have changed in that time." He doesn't need to tell me what they're hinting at. Mariah's dad could be shot tonight. "Keep me posted, officer."

"Yes, sir."

I hang up and walk back inside. I sit next to DJ and pull my girl into my lap. "How are you doing, beautiful girl?"

She burrows into me, but says nothing. I reach up to her neck to feel her pulse. She's calmed down considerably.

"Matt?"

"Yeah, Lyric. I'm here."

"Don't leave her alone tonight."

"Not a chance in hell I'm ever leaving her alone again."

"Good."

I kiss Mariah on the head and hold her tightly.

DJ looks at me as he stands. "Brody said he'd make it into a call for the last two hours of our shift so we don't lose time."

"I talked to him on the way here. But you know I wouldn't give a shit."

"We know. Both of us. But we take care of our own. You know that." He gives Mariah's shoulder a squeeze as he waits for me to give him my radio and body camera. "Lyric is calmed down. She's okay. Mariah is okay. She just needs to be kept far away from all of that shit. She needs you."

"Thank you, Lyric. For everything," I say.

"You're welcome."

DJ takes his phone and leans down to hug Mariah. "I'll head out."

"DJ?" Mariah asks weakly.

"Yeah, sweetheart?"

"Make sure Lyric is okay."

75

"Don't worry. I'll take care of Lyric," he says. He kisses her on top of the head and heads out.

I lift Mariah up and carry her to my apartment. She doesn't try to fight me. She wraps her arms around my shoulders and melts into me. My sister, who's just dropping off the kids at what would be the end of my shift and beginning of hers, gives me a wide-eyed surprised look. She knows about Mariah, but hasn't met her yet.

"Not now, Liz. Can you lock up?"

She nods as she stands and gets ready to leave. I carry Mariah to my bedroom. I set her down gently on the end of the bed and find a t-shirt for her to wear. She takes it without a word and heads for the bathroom. I start taking off my gear; putting my guns in my gun safe.

After checking on the kids, making sure they're tucked into bed and asleep, I crawl into my bed as Mariah walks back into my bedroom wearing my t-shirt. She looks broken.

"Come here, baby."

She crawls into the bed. I wrap her up in the blanket and in my arms. She molds herself to me. "What happened to my dad?"

"They have a team trying to get him out. Officer Howard will call me with news."

"You?"

"I'm not letting them call you anymore with this. Let me handle it." She nods, and that's how I know she's exhausted. She doesn't attempt an argument. "I don't want you alone at night anymore. From now on, you sleep here, or I sleep at your place. No more you being alone. I know you're tired right now because your attacks sap your strength, but we're setting rules tomorrow."

"Okay."

I kiss her cheek. "Go to sleep, baby."

"Okay."

I hug her tightly.

"Matt?"

"Yeah?"

"Don't let me go."

"Not a chance in hell."

She shifts slightly and puts her arm around my waist. Within seconds, she's asleep.

A few minutes later, I get a text about Mariah's dad being okay and taken to the hospital for a psych hold. Sleep doesn't come easy to me. My mind races, and all I can think about is how I am never letting her go through this again.

I don't know how long I lay in bed before exhaustion finally overtakes me.

Chapter Nine

✫ Mariah ✫

The first thing I feel when I wake up is a pounding headache. Almost like an entire band of trolls has started playing behind my left eye.

I try to force myself to open my eyes. The second thing I feel is an instant wave of nausea. I snap my eyes immediately closed and attempt breathing through my nose.

I don't want to throw up. I hate throwing up. Throwing up is a horrible, horrible fate that I am positive is the only true way to win a war. Make the enemy throw up. War would instantaneously go away. The world would be thrown into peace because no one wants to throw up so violently that they die. Or... almost die.

After taking several deep breaths, I make an attempt to move. Matt isn't in the bed so I know it's after seven in the morning. And despite everything that happened yesterday, I need to know what happened to my dad. I slowly open my eyes and look around for my phone. I know Matt put it on the nightstand near his bed. I saw him do it, but it isn't there.

I make a slow and cautious attempt to stand. Panic attacks always exhaust me, but the really bad ones... The really bad ones make me feel like it would be better for me to jump off a roof than go through the day.

The nausea. The migraine. The chest pain. The overwhelming need to go to sleep for the entire day. It's all so much.

After deciding I'm not going to fall on my ass if I walk, I take a few cautious steps to the door. I slowly open it and make my way to the living room.

"Mariah!" Marie says.

I wince and my hand inevitably goes straight to my head as Marie and Brit crash into me, enveloping me in a huge hug. Beckett grins from his stack of Legos on the floor.

"You're finally awake!" Brit says.

I fight the nausea with a deep breath and force myself to hug them back. "Hey, sweeties. How was your sleep? Good dreams?" I ask quietly.

They drag me to the couch and push me to sit down. The world flips upside down, and I close my eyes as someone crawls into my lap.

"I had a dream that I was riding a unicorn. A pink one with sparkles," Marie says.

"Rainbow sparkles?" I ask.

I open my eyes as Marie giggles and starts playing with my hair.

"Girls? I don't think Mariah's feeling so well. Let's be a little quieter for her, okay?"

I look up to see a beautiful woman sitting down next to me as the girls climb off of me. She's gorgeous. She has the most beautiful green eyes and dark blond hair. She looks near the same age as Matt, and I vaguely recognize her from somewhere, but I'm not sure where.

The kids sit down on the floor in front of me and start to color. I fight another wave of nausea and stabbing pain in my head. The woman puts her hand comfortingly on my arm.

"Matt told me to give you these. And to make you drink a shake because he knows you won't be able to hold any food down."

I look at her and smile softly as she hands me two pills and a glass with a white substance in it. I take the pills and a cautious sip of the shake.

"It's... actually kind of good. I expected something gross and gritty."

The woman laughs softly. "Yeah, he really likes his protein shakes. I don't know how he drinks them. But he promised this one wouldn't be like that."

79

I take another sip, surprised it's actually calming my stomach. "Um… I'm sorry if this is rude, but who are you? And where's Matt?"

She smiles. "I seem to have you at a bit of a disadvantage, don't I?" I smile a little and focus on the shake. "I'm Elizabeth. I'm Matt's sister."

I instantly go white and frown as my eyes widen. I reach down to tug the end of Matt's shirt down. It's all I'm wearing other than a pair of pink silky panties. This is not the first impression I wanted to make when I met his sister. Oh God.

She softly laughs again and smiles at me. Her laugh is infectious and, for some reason, she actually makes me feel calm. "It's okay, Mariah. You don't need to be shy."

I give her a weak smile as I continue slowly drinking my shake. "Um… I was looking for my phone. I thought it was in the bedroom."

"Well, it was. Matt wanted to make sure that you weren't disturbed this morning. So he gave it to me with strict orders to only let you contact your friend Lyric, DJ, or him." I raise an eyebrow, and Elizabeth reads me like a book. "He's not trying to be controlling. He just wants to make sure you don't get sent into another panic attack."

I nod slightly, the movement sending my head reeling. I close my eyes again. "Where is he anyway?"

"He had a callout last night. Not long after he brought you here. He left about four this morning. He didn't want to leave you, but there was a kid involved. None of those guys can resist when a kid is involved. I was at work, but I came here as soon as I was able to get off."

I glance at the clock. It's nearly ten in the morning.

I sigh and finish my shake, feeling the familiar pain in my chest. I don't know what happened to my dad. I don't know if Lyric is okay. I need to. I don't want to bother Matt, and I doubt he would've told Lyric how my dad is. Not knowing, though, is hard. Really, really hard.

I rub my chest as I stand and walk to the kitchen. As I rinse out my cup, I wince again. The stabbing pain in my chest and head is overwhelming.

I feel Elizabeth start rubbing my back. "Are you okay, honey?"

Tears sting my eyes, I shake my head. I keep my voice low so the kids don't hear. "I need to know what happened to my dad. I don't know who to call. I don't want to bother Matt. I don't know if he would have told my friend, Lyric. And I don't know how Lyric is. She was upset and just as panicky as me last night. And I'm starting to get panicked about not knowing."

Before she can respond, the door opens and Matt walks in. "Hey, rugrats!"

"Matt!" Brit says.

"Matty!" Marie exclaims.

"Hey, Uncle Matt!" Beckett says.

The girls run to him, and he picks them both up. I turn away and force myself to breathe as Elizabeth rubs my back.

"What are you girls doing?" Matt asks.

"Drawing," Brit says.

"Why don't you two draw Mariah a picture that she can frame and hang on her wall? I have to talk to her, okay?"

"Okay!" Marie yells. My head nearly implodes.

Moments later, Matt's strong arms wrap around me. He kisses the side of my head and takes my hand. He leads me to his bedroom and closes the door behind us. "Talk to me, Rih." He sits down on the edge of the bed and pulls me onto his lap. "What happened? I know the signs of an attack by now."

I sniffle and lean my head on his shoulder. His arms encircle my waist. "You took my phone. I understand why, but I don't know what happened to my dad. I don't know if Lyric is okay. And I need to. Not knowing is causing me to panic."

He gently lifts my face to his and softly kisses me. "My sister had your phone. Did you look at it?" I shake my head and bite my lip. "Hmm... You didn't get to talk to Lyric. And you didn't call or text me."

"No. I didn't want to bother you, and I didn't think Lyric would know how my dad is doing. I didn't think you'd tell her. I don't know if you even have her number, so you don't have a way to get ahold of her unless you message her from my phone. I don't know how she's doing. Your sister said -"

"Honey, stop. Take a deep breath." He hands me my phone as I take a deep breath. "I sent you a text this morning so you would see right away what happened. I had DJ give me Lyric's number. I told him last night, and I texted Lyric, too. I know she was just as worried as you." He shows me the text he sent to me.

81

Matt: Good morning, baby. Just want you to know, so you don't worry. They got your dad into a psych hold last night. He's okay. And I know you'll worry about Lyric. Check your messages from her.

I do just that. Lyric says she's okay. That DJ talked her down. Matt filled her in on what happened with my dad. She said everything is still on track to her moving here. She'll be here within the week. She's excited and can't wait to be here. I laugh softly when she says I should be prepared to be tackled. Matt and DJ, too. I have no doubt she and DJ will disappear quickly.

"Matt..."

"I'm not your ex, beautiful. I'm far different. I'm not your dad. I care about you. I'll always be here for you."

He takes my phone and nudges me off him. He tosses my phone on the bed and stands up to remove his gun and equipment. After he has everything put away and he's changed, he gets into his bed and pulls me in with him.

"Take off the t-shirt."

I look at him incredulously. "What? Matt, I'm not... ready for -"

"Rih. Take... off... the... shirt... I'm not going to do anything. You have got to learn to trust me."

I shakily take off the shirt, and his eyes rake over my body, leaving heat in its wake. He smiles softly and pats the bed next to him. "On your stomach."

"Um... o-okay." I lay on my stomach next to him and his large, warm hand finds the small of my back. He starts rubbing my back and neck. I groan as the tension and the anxiety slowly leave my body. "Oh my God." He leans down and kisses my shoulder and the back of my head as his fingers curl in my hair. He starts rubbing the back of my head. I nearly purr "Never stop."

The low chuckle that escapes his lips rumbles in his chest. "I told you that you could trust me, baby."

"I do. Really." I turn my head towards him.

"I'd never do anything to hurt you. I won't do anything you don't want me to."

82

He leans down to meet my lips as he rubs my back. His lips are both soft and commanding. In seconds, our kiss has turned wild. His tongue takes complete control, and I relinquish it to him.

He groans as his hand slides down to my bottom. I turn to him and press against him, my naked and aching breasts against his hard chest. I run my fingers softly against the well-defined ridges of his perfect abs. He squeezes my ass and wraps his other arm around me, effectively pulling me closer to him.

"Matt...," I whimper into his mouth as he runs his hand up my rib cage and grabs my breast in his hand. "Mmm..."

"God that feels better than I dreamed." He pinches my nipple between his fingers. I gasp. "You like that?"

"Yes. God, yes..."

He pushes me onto my back. He's rough and commanding, but still gentle with me. He straddles me and leans down to kiss me as he takes both of my wrists in his hands. He pins both of them above my head and takes one of my breasts in his other hand. He massages it gently as he kisses me. I arch into him as he grabs my nipple and pinches and pulls it.

"Mmm... Oooohhh..." I squirm against him as he continues to play with it. He kisses down my neck to my other breast and flicks his tongue across it. "Oh!"

He stops and looks up at me. "You gotta be quiet, baby. My sister and the kids are out there."

I nod. He smiles as he goes back to lavishing my nipples with attention. He switches the hand holding my wrists and flicks his tongue across my other nipple while he rubs the one his mouth just left. He lightly bites.

I can't help the cry that escapes. "Oh!"

He stops and looks up at me again. He smiles and shakes his head as he gets up, pulling me up hard by my wrists. He keeps hold of my wrists with one hand as his other caresses my cheek.

"What did I just say?"

I can't form words. All I can think about is him. His hard cock against my stomach as he pins me against him. His incredible dominance.

He takes my chin between his fingers and forces me to look at him. My breath quickens. "I asked you a question, Mariah." His voice is deep and commanding.

"T-to stay quiet."

"And did you?"

"N-no."

I love this. I love this playful side. This dominant side. I've never been dominated before. It excites me in the craziest of ways.

"No, what?"

I see the gleam in his eye. He's enjoying this as much as me. "No..." I look him in his gorgeous coffee colored eyes and bite my lip as I give him a sweet smile. "Sergeant."

I see the moment the playful look in his eye turns to heat and want. Lust. I feel his cock twitch against me.

Hmm... He likes being called Sergeant.

He gives me a sexy smirk and pushes me back on the bed. Still straddling me, he runs his hands over my breasts, down my stomach and to my hips. He grips them hard, and flips me over to my stomach.

"Get up on all fours."

I slowly, and as sexily as possible, do as he says. He bends over me, his hardness against my ass. He wraps my hair around his hand as he pushes me down. My head is against the pillows, and my ass is in the air for him. He kisses down my back and lets go of my hair. His hands grip my hips once more. I feel one of them run softly across my back until he gets to my panty line. He grips the waistband and pulls. The fabric covering my pussy hits every nerve that craves his touch.

"Matt!"

He pulls back from me, and I whimper.

"Again? Didn't I just tell you to be quiet?" His hand comes down hard on the globe of my ass. I cry out into the pillow. His hand comes down hard again on my other cheek. I cry out into the pillow again. His hand rubs and squeezes both cheeks before coming down hard again.

Holy shit. Why does that feel so good?

He spanks me again. I grip the sheets as I cry out again into the pillows. The sting from his hand sends unbelievable want and need low in my stomach. The feeling both confuses the hell out of me and makes me want him to touch me more than I want to breathe.

He rubs his hand across the sting, then leans over me. He takes both breasts in his hands and whispers in my ear. "What do good girls say when they do something wrong and they know it?"

84

"I'm sorry."

"I'm sorry what?" He drags his teeth across my shoulder, then licks it.

"I'm sorry, Sergeant." I feel him smile against my neck as he gets up. He slowly runs his hands down my stomach to my panty line again. He slides his hand over my panties and gives me a little pressure. I moan and push myself back into his cock. He grabs my panty line and pulls again, rubbing them between my slit.

This. This must be what Lyric was talking about when she said I had to experience it on my own.

"Oh God... Matt...," I whisper, trying to abide by his rules. He rubs himself against me. His boxer briefs are far too much clothing between us. I want him naked. "Please? Matt, please."

"What do you want, beautiful?"

"You. I want you. Please?" I need him. I'm not ashamed to beg him for it.

"Not with the kids and Liz out there. Our first time, I'm going to make you scream my name, Mariah."

I whimper. The teasing. The touching. The spanking. The feel of him. I'm going crazy. He pulls up on my panties again, and I cry out into the pillow.

"Such a good girl." He pulls my panties down to my knees. I move to wiggle out of them, but he holds me still. "Nope. Panties stay right where they are." He runs a finger between my slick slit, and I grip the sheets again.

Finally. Oh my God. Finally. We've been together for somewhere near two months. Maybe just over one. I've lost track, but we've never been more intimate than making out. I wanted to take things slowly, and he respected that. But I'm ready. I may have just said I'm not, but that was fear talking. I want him.

"Mmm..."

"Is this what you want, baby?"

"Yes. Please? Please..." He rubs my clit and runs his finger up and down from my pussy to my clit slowly again.

"Yes please what?" He slowly removes his finger. I can hear him suck on it.

"Yes please, Sergeant."

85

He slips his wet finger back between my slit and rubs my clit again. "Good girl."

He slides his finger inside me. I scream out into the pillow. His long finger strokes me, hitting all of my sensitive places. I try to move with his finger, but he holds me still.

"Oh my God, Matt..."

He slips another finger inside me, filling me. "Feel good, baby?"

"Yes... Yes. So good." I grind against his fingers the best I can with him holding me still. I've never been fingered like this before. It's always hard. Fast. And when I didn't come, I was given up on.

He starts moving faster and deeper. "Yes what?"

"Yes, Sergeant."

"You're so wet for me."

I've never had anyone make me come before. Just myself. As soon as his thumb touches my clit, I feel an incredible tingle. Familiar, yet not. It feels so much better than when I'm touching myself. It quickly turns into a raging inferno, and my legs start shaking.

"Matt... Oh my God... I think… I'm..."

"You think what?"

"I think I'm gonna come... I've never… Not... for… anyone… Just me."

I feel him crook his fingers inside me and give my clit pressure. "Come for me, pretty girl."

I shatter as I scream into the pillows. My stomach clenches. I squeeze hard and pulse around his fingers. He slows his pace inside me, helping me come down, until the spasming stops. He slowly pulls out his fingers and moves to my side. He lays down and pulls me into his arms.

He sticks both fingers in his mouth and sucks them. "You taste incredibly sweet, baby girl." I feel my cheeks turn hot as he leans down to kiss me. "What do you need? Water? Anything?"

"Actually, water would be nice," I whisper. My throat is dry and sore from the screaming and moaning.

He kisses me again and gets up to get the water from his private master bathroom. I take a long drink, but he grabs my wrist and gently lowers the cup from my lips.

"Sip it. Gulping it like that is never good for you."

I nod and take another sip before handing the cup back to him. He puts the cup on the nightstand before he crawls back into bed. He wraps us both in the blanket and then pulls me close to him.

"No one's ever made me come before." I hide in his chest, refusing to look at him. "I've only ever been with two people, but neither of them have ever done that before. I've... only come one time... for myself... I didn't really do it much. And one time no one touched me."

He looks down at me, curiously. "Well, now I need to know."

My cheeks flush. "I got really turned on reading something... And imagining it was you and I in the roles."

"You got so turned on you came without touching yourself?"

"Um... Yeah. Lyric was telling me about her first night with DJ. You were in my bedroom putting the dresser together."

I bury my face in his chest, and he hugs me tighter. "Ah... I see. I'll admit that it sounded like it was a pretty hot night. I got a little turned on when DJ told me." I look up at him in surprise. He leans down to kiss me with a chuckle. "Well, I can't say I'm upset that I'm the first to make you come while touching you. And now that I know that, my new goal is to make you come every night, because seeing you unravel like that is the hottest thing I've ever seen."

I can't help but laugh as I look up at him. I reach up and run my palm over his cheek as I take a deep breath. I have to ask. I need to know.

"Um... so... are you like... a dom? And into really crazy sex stuff?"

He looks at me in astonishment, then laughs. I bite my lip and look down at his chest.

He catches my face and forces me to look at him. "I'm not into BDSM and all that crazy kink shit. I like control in the bedroom. I like to use my cuffs, but I won't tie you up or blindfold you or whip you. Nothing like that. And a little punishment when you mouth off or do something I said not to isn't a bad thing, is it?"

I smile and shake my head. "No."

"You seemed to like it just as much as I did. Right?"

"Right," I say softly.

He kisses me. "If you don't like it, or if I'm being too rough, tell me. I'll never ever do something you're uncomfortable with. I use safewords. If you can't think of one, you can use red. I'll stop right away

87

as soon as you say it. You can say it when you're uncomfortable, or if something hurts you, or if you want me to stop what I'm doing because you don't like it. Understand?"

I nod. "I think so."

"Do you have a safeword in mind?"

I think for a moment. "Um… Onion. I hate onions."

He gives me a cocky smile. "Onion it is. I promise you. Giving me control will be pleasurable for both of us."

I laugh and bury my head in his chest. He kisses the top of my head as I lazily rub his back. I smile when I feel his breathing even out. I follow behind him moments later and fall asleep in his arms.

Chapter Ten

★ Matt ★

(One Year Later)

Over the past year, Mariah and I have fallen into a sexy and very comfortable routine. If Elizabeth is working, Mariah stays at my place with me and the kids. She's there if I'm working or get called out. On days that I'm not working, and I don't have Elizabeth's kids, I stay with her. Things with DJ and Lyric are incredible. They both seem as happy as me and Mariah. Mariah has another book out. This one ended up a bestseller. Things between us are perfect. Every day we spend together is better than the last.

And nearly every single night, Mariah is underneath me. Her legs wrapped around my waist and her nails digging into my back is one of the best feelings in the world.

It's after three in the morning, and I'm just coming home from my shift. I quietly and quickly let myself into Mariah's apartment, locking up behind me. I smile to myself when I see my girl sprawled across her bed naked on top of her blankets. She hasn't gotten used to the Florida heat yet.

She consistently complains that the heat is suffocating. Even in the air conditioning.

I start taking off my gear when I hear her rustling behind me. I turn around as I'm unbuttoning my uniform shirt.

She's sitting up in her bed looking at me. "It's so hot. I don't know how you survive it," she says sleepily to me.

"Baby, is it really that different from Minnesota?"

"Yes. The average temp is like seventy two in July. Here, I'm lucky if it's below eighty. And even though we're not right on the ocean, there's still humidity. It's awful." I laugh and shake my head as I turn back to her closet to finish putting my stuff away. "I bought you something," she says.

"Oh yeah?"

"It's on the top shelf. Where you put your gun."

"You mean, you were actually able to reach the top shelf?"

"Shut-up."

We both laugh. I love teasing her about her height, but honestly it's one of the sexiest things about her. I've never dated a woman who was less than five feet seven or something. But she's only five feet three. I had no idea how attractive height could be until I had her in my arms. I not only tower over her, but I engulf her. She fits with me like she was made for me.

I reach up to the top shelf and find a metal box. "Is it this box up here? The metal one?" I ask her as I grab it.

"Mmhmm... There's a key taped to the top."

I take my flashlight out so I don't blind her by turning on the light as I open the box.

"A gun safe?" I grin like a schoolboy.

"For your service weapon. I know you feel uncomfortable with it not being locked away when you're here. Even though you trust me with it."

My heart swells with love for her. She knows me so well. She can read my wants and needs like no one I've ever been with.

I put my gun and everything else away, then climb naked into bed with her. I pull her close and kiss her.

"Thank you, baby."

"You're welcome."

90

She lightly traces my abs with her fingertip, and I smile as I wrap her hair around my hand. "Want something?" I ask.

"You."

I laugh. She doesn't hold back with me. I love that she's not afraid to tell me what she wants. "Oh yeah?"

"Yeah. I want you." She reaches down and grabs my length. She squeezes and starts stroking.

I suck in a breath. "Fuck..." I reach down and grab her wrist, releasing myself from her hand, even though everything in me screams in protest. "You know that's not how things work. Did I tell you that you could start stroking me?"

"Mmm... No..." She leans into me and tries to kiss me, but I grin and pull back. "No fair."

"What am I going to do with you? You're such a brat."

She laughs. "I can think of a few things." She tries to kiss me again, but I hold her back. I love playing like this with her.

"You're really asking for it tonight, aren't you?" I say as my eyes darken with all of the want I feel for her.

"Maybe... What are you going to do about it?"

I growl and pull her out of bed. I bend her over the bed. She wiggles her ass. I squeeze it. "Don't move."

"Yes, Sergeant."

I smile like a damn fool as I walk to my bag. I find my cuffs and a key and walk back to her. I put the key on her dresser and slowly run my hand up her back, wrapping her hair around my fist. I tug her up to me. She hits my chest with her back and gasps.

I bend down to whisper in her ear. "Hands behind your back."

"What?" She shivers with anticipation as I run my hands down her arms.

"You heard me, trouble."

She puts her hands behind her back and tries to grab my cock. I growl and swat her hand as I gently bite her neck. I slap the cuffs on her wrists and quickly double lock them so they don't hurt her.

"Matt... What are you doing?"

We've never used the cuffs before, but she's ready. "You'll see." I push her down so she's bent over the bed and use my foot to spread her legs. "So insistent on disobeying." I swat her ass.

91

"Oh God. Yes…," she moans. I run my cock along her clit, and then pull back. She whimpers. "Matt. Please..."

I swat her ass again, and she screams into the blanket. I tease her a little more with my cock. "Is this what you're looking for?" I dip a finger inside her. "Is this what has you so dripping wet for me?"

"Yes! Please... Please!" She pushes herself back into me, but I hold her hips steady as I pull out and away from her.

I swat her ass again. I love when she screams out. "Yes please what?"

"Yes please, Sergeant."

"Good girl." I swat her again.

"Oh! I'm sorry. I'm sorry, Sergeant. I'm sorry."

"For what?" I rub my hand along the globe of her ass. "What are you sorry for?" I give her a couple squeezes as I continue to rub away the sting my hand left.

"For trying to take control…." She looks back at me and bites her lip. I grin and reach down between her legs. I slide two fingers inside her and feel her instantly constrict around me. "Oh yes. Yes… So, so good!"

I set my thumb against her clit, and she starts shaking. I pull out. "You don't think I am going to let you come that fast, do you?"

I pull her up to me by the cuffs and reach around to rub my hands over her breasts. She moans. I run my hands down her stomach to her dripping wet pussy. I hold her close and tightly against me as I bend to kiss her neck. I run my teeth and tongue over her shoulder as I dip two fingers inside her again.

"Ah!... Mmm..." She throws her head back against me as I, once again, set my thumb against her clit. I feel her stomach quiver. Her legs shake as her breath quickens, so I pull out once more. "No... You're killing me."

"Making you pout is so fucking hot, though." I guide her in front of me by the cuffs to the wall next to the dresser, and then turn her around and push her against it. I reach down and lift her. Her legs wrap tightly around my back, but she flails a little. Unsteady. "Mariah. Trust me." I hold her between me and the wall and feel her relax. "I've got you. You don't need to hold onto me. Trust me."

I guide her onto my hard, waiting cock, and she completely relaxes. "Mmm..."

92

"That's my good girl."

"That… feels so good."

"See?" After she adjusts to my size, I start moving inside her, slowly and deeply.

"Oh my God. So good."

I pin her harder against the wall and quicken my pace. Her legs tighten around me. I kiss her as she meets my thrusts.

"I told you." I grab the key from her dresser and unlock the cuffs. They fall to the floor as I step away from the wall, turning and throwing her onto the bed.

"Matt!"

I grab her hips and yank her down to me, reentering her in one sure thrust. "Fuck, Rih. You're so tight. So wet for me."

"That's because you keep teasing me."

I grin. If I didn't need to be inside her, I'd tease her more. Instead, I grab her legs and put them up on my shoulders, effectively lifting her hips off the mattress and driving myself deeply inside her. She grips the mattress tightly.

"Oh… You like that?" I pull out and drive as deeply inside her as I can over and over. I know her. I know how much she likes it.

"I'm close. So close…"

"You think I can't feel how close you are, beautiful?"

"Please…"

"Please what?" I keep driving into her with more and more intensity.

"Please, Sergeant…"

I reach down and rub circles around her clit. "That's my good girl. Come for me, baby."

She clenches so hard around me, she nearly rips my own orgasm from me. I pinch her clit between my fingers, and she releases. "Oh! Matt… Oh my…"

I collapse on top of her and let myself release. "Shit. Holy shit, baby. You're so fucking good."

We lay with each other while I empty into her and her pussy squeezes around me as she comes. Her fingers run through my hair as I lay my head on her breasts. After a few moments, I kiss between them and slowly pull out of her as I get up. We crawl into bed and she curls up in my

93

arms. I leave the blanket off of us as I pull her close to me. She's asleep almost instantly, and I follow closely behind her.

★★★

I jerk awake at the insistent buzzing coming from Mariah's speaker box. I groan as I open my eyes. It's only six in the morning. We've been asleep for maybe an hour after we went to bed.

"Fuck," I groan. Mariah whimpers as I get out of bed. "I know, baby. I'll be right back." She curls up and covers her head with the blankets. I smile at how fucking adorable she is.

I get to the speaker box and wait for it to buzz again. My glare turns more and more vicious as the minutes tick by. It's probably some drunk asshole trying to be stupidly funny. Just when I think whoever it is is done fucking around, it buzzes again.

"What?" I growl, pushing the speaker button. Nothing. Of course nothing. I wait for any type of sounds, but get nothing. I'm more and more convinced that it's some drunk college student. After another few moments, I push the button again. "Touch that button again, I will come down there, arrest you, and throw your ass in detox."

I let go of the button and wait a few more minutes before going back to the bedroom. I'm just laying down when I see my phone is buzzing. I growl low under my breath, careful not to wake Mariah. No reason for her to be up when she has the option of sleep.

"Is the entire universe out to make sure I don't get a second of fucking sleep today?" I mumble quietly as I get back out of the bed. I answer, closing the bedroom door softly behind me. "What the fuck do you want?"

"I know it's early. I'm just as tired as you," DJ grumbles. I look at my phone and see his name on the caller ID. I hadn't bothered to look at my screen before I answered.

"Why are you calling me so fucking early? We both got off shift at the same time, and if Lyric is as much like Mariah as you say she is, I know you've only gotten about an hour of sleep like I did."

94

"I haven't gotten any sleep. We were laying down when I got a call from Brody. He said he couldn't get ahold of you. He's been trying for an hour."

"Fuck, I was out. Both of us, I guess. Usually Mariah hears my phone vibrating if I don't."

"It doesn't matter, Matt. Listen. Me and Lyric are on the way over there right now."

I shake my head, feeling like I'm coming out of a fog. "What? Why?"

"Because Blake pulled Mariah's dad over. Ran his name and saw your alert come up."

I sit down and deflate. I was really hoping this would never happen. Around a week ago, Mariah started getting phone calls from her father again. He told her he refused to allow her to interfere in his life anymore. We had no idea what he was talking about. Mariah hadn't had anything to do with him since the night he had been picked up by the Duluth Police Department for a seventy-two hour psych hold.

He had called her after he was released. We were at DJ's son's party. We both saw her expression change when she answered and both immediately made a beeline for her. DJ took her phone and put it on speaker after he led us into a private room. Lyric saw what was happening and followed us, concerned. Her dad yelled and screamed at her accusing her of stealing his dog and killing him. None of us could believe what we were hearing. After that, though, we hadn't heard from him again.

Until about a week ago.

I blocked his number on her phone immediately, but he was still able to leave voicemails. Stupid, ridiculous shit about how he knew where she lived. How he was going to make sure she couldn't do anything to fuck with his life anymore. I didn't put much credibility to what he was saying, but I was concerned enough to put an alert on him. If he showed up in Gainesville and had any contact with the police department, I'd be notified.

The problem was that unless he had contact with any of the officers, be it in a traffic stop or showing up at the department for some dumb reason, I wouldn't have any idea he was here. I started getting more concerned about him when he started emailing Mariah and contacting her on her social media accounts about the same things. He knew where she

95

lived. He planned on making the trip and making sure she couldn't bother him anymore.

It was enough to make me get a harassment order started for her. I have the paperwork all filled out sitting on Mariah's counter. All I need to do is bring it to the courthouse and wait for them to get her a hearing and approve it. Then if he contacts her, I can get him thrown in jail.

"Matt?" Mariah says sleepily from the door to the bedroom. I look up, trying to hide the pained expression on my face. "What's wrong? Come back to bed." She yawns and blinks sleepily.

"Mariah, uh…" I'm cut off by a loud pounding on the door. "Fuck." The pounding gets louder and more insistent.

Mariah furrows her eyebrows and starts walking to the door. "Who could that be at this hour?"

My heart stops beating. I leap up and cross the room in only a couple strides. I grab her arm and yank her back against my chest as I move with her back to the bedroom. I push her gently but forcefully into the room. She gives me the most bewildered expression I've ever seen, and I hate that I can't explain it to her. There's no time. I hand her my phone.

"Please just stay in here. Please. DJ is on the phone. Please stay in here for me." I kiss her before I tug the door closed. If I could lock it from the outside, I would. But I'll have to trust my girl. I'll have to trust that she trusts me enough to listen to me.

I don't know what I'm about to open that door to, but if the furious knocking is any indication, I know the next few minutes are going to be fucking intense. But I won't let him near her. I won't let him touch my girl.

Chapter Eleven

☆ Mariah ☆

I stumble back into the room confused and astonished that Matt just pushed me in here. I contemplate opening the door but stop myself. Above and beyond everything that just happened and how bewildered I am, I trust my boyfriend. He has a reason for everything, and I've learned not to question him.

Remembering I have the phone in my hand, I bring it up to my ear. "DJ?" I ask shakily.

"We're on our way, sweetheart. Here. Talk to Lyric. I'm racing through the streets to get to you. I don't want to crash."

"What? DJ, what's happening?" Knowing DJ is racing through the streets to get here freaks me out. "DJ!"

"Mariah? It's okay. We're coming," Lyric says softly.

"Lyric, what the hell is going on? No one will talk to me. Matt just shoved me into the bedroom and told me not to come out, and DJ won't tell me. He never keeps anything from me. Something is happening. Please tell me."

"I... Mariah. It's... It's your -" I don't hear the rest of Lyric's sentence as raised voices catch my attention. I could have sworn that sounded like… I shake my head at the thought. It can't be. He's fifteen hundred miles away from me.

I move slowly towards the door to listen. My breath catches, and I'm over taken with a sense of dread. He can't be here. He can't. But I know instinctively that it is. All of the voicemails and emails and messages on my Instagram and Facebook... They all come back to me.

"He knows… He knows where I am. Oh… God." I fight to breathe.

"Mariah? Talk to me!" Lyric pleads. I barely register her. All of my attention is focused on the voices beyond the door.

"I know this is her apartment!"

"Mr. Peterson, with all due respect, you aren't getting anywhere near her."

I can't stay in here. My heart is racing as I listen. I can hear him getting more worked up. I need to help. I need to calm him down before he hurts himself. Before he tries to hurt Matt. I open the door a crack. The voices are so much louder now, and a fight within my own mind begins. Should I go out there? Should I trust that Matt can handle himself and my father?

The sound of a scuffle makes the decision for me as I unconsciously move out of the bedroom, just enough to see around the corner to the front door. My father is trying to shove past Matt. Our eyes meet, and I swallow.

Hard.

His eyes widen, before they narrow at me. His lips curl into a snarl. "Mariah!" He starts fighting even harder to get past Matt. To get to me. My heart races, and I take a couple steps back with wide, frightened eyes as I watch Matt struggle to get a good grip on him. To hold him back. To keep him from me.

His eyes are wild. His grin is maniacal. The growls and grunts are feral. His bared teeth are monstrous. I barely register Lyric screaming as I drop the phone. My eyes are fixated on the crazed man wrestling with Matt.

"Mariah! Go back into the bedroom!" Matt grunts with the effort of holding my dad back. He can't get a grip on him. My dad's jerky movements are making him unpredictable. Every time Matt pushes him back, he pushes forward harder.

I vaguely hear shouts in the background as Lyric appears in the doorway with DJ close behind her. Brody is right behind them. Lyric pauses fearfully in the doorway watching the struggle before focusing her attention on me. She starts to run towards me, but DJ grabs her around the waist from behind, lifting her off the ground and taking a few steps back before she has the chance to take more than a step towards me.

"Lyric! Stop!" DJ yells, holding her tight to him as Brody shoves by both of them to help Matt.

My head is spinning, and I feel nauseous. Like I'm on a Tilt-A-Whirl. The ground beneath me is unsteady, and I feel like I'm trying to stay upright in the middle of an earthquake. Everything around me feels like it's going in slow motion. I reach out for something… anything to steady me. Anchor me.

Matt is on the ground holding my father off him. Brody is fighting to get a strong grip. There's yelling.

Screaming.

I can hear my own heartbeat pounding in my ears like the engine of an F-18 fighter jet.

"DJ! Let go! Mariah needs me!" Lyric screams. I force myself to focus. If I don't focus on something, I'll pass out. Lyric cries and struggles against DJ as she tries desperately to get to me. She can see I'm on the verge of a full panic attack, and I love that she cares enough to want to help. I watch as DJ holds Lyric tightly to his chest, swaying with her to calm her. He's whispering something in her ear. Her head is tilted slightly to one side, so I know she is listening, though she's focused completely on me. I can see her calming.

"Fuck! Get off!" Matt shoves my father off him as Brody heaves him up. They both work together to subdue him, and haul him out of the apartment. As soon as they're out, DJ lets Lyric go. She doesn't hesitate. She races towards me as my legs give out. I try to catch myself on a wall or anything, but there's nothing around me.

"Mariah!" Lyric's eyes widen as she shouts while I start going down. DJ is a blur of motion as he sprints for me. He catches me just before I hit the ground, lifting me in his arms like a modern day Superman. He drops on the couch with me in his lap and hugs me tightly to his chest.

99

All of the fight whooshes out of me like air in a balloon. I collapse against him and burrow into his chest. Lyric wraps her arms around me just as tightly as DJ has. Both of them rock in harmony with me.

"It's okay, Mariah. We're here. We're right here," Lyric whispers. She runs her fingers soothingly through my hair as DJ runs his hand up and down my back.

I breathe in DJ's fresh, earthy, masculine scent, thanking my lucky stars that he's here, and he brought Lyric. Even though I know there is no way she would have stayed behind. She would have found her way here, with or without DJ.

Although, I don't know that she would have moved here from the United Kingdom as quickly as she had if she hadn't fallen in love with him. I like to think she would have.

I'm still not sure how it all happened so quickly. For some reason, DJ took a liking to her. They talked online and in text every single day since the day they met on Skype when he was helping to get me unpacked and arrange furniture. Once she realized she was falling for him, she reached out to me. She was unsure. She'd been hurt before and was hesitant. She needed my reassurance. My approval in a way. My blessing.

Within a couple of months, she was moving here and in with DJ. I couldn't have been any more happy for either of them if I had tried. They were perfect for each other. They needed each other. She brings out his playful side. He tames her wild side.

"You're okay, Mariah," DJ whispers. I put my ear against his chest as Lyric molds herself to my back. Between the two of them, my breathing slows. I become more steady.

"Where's Matt?" I ask after a few minutes.

"Him and Brody are making sure your father leaves the property. They'll get a couple of on duty officers to deal with him, then come back up here."

"I don't want to stay here. I don't want to live in this apartment building. How did he get in? It's a secured building."

"I don't know, honey," DJ says as he continues hugging me tightly.

"Maybe you could stay with us for awhile," Lyric suggests, tugging my hair lightly.

"There's no other option. I'll talk to Matt. We'll get some things packed. You're both coming home with us until we can regroup and figure out where to go from here."

All I can do is nod and let the two of them hug me. I don't feel safe here. He's ruined my little sanctuary I'd built. He's ruined the sense of safety I'd created. No matter how far I get from him, he continues to find ways to ruin my life.

☆☆☆

(One Month Later)

It takes me a second after I wake up to realize someone is knocking softly on the bedroom door. I try to get up, but Matt holds me tightly. I try to gently push him off so I can move.

"Mariah? Matt? Are you awake?" Lyric asks, calling softly through the door. We'd been staying with them for nearly a month now. Matt and I had bought a house, but we're waiting for it to close. Neither of us felt safe going back to the apartment building.

"Babe, Lyric's at the door. I have to get up," I say softly, nuzzling his cheek.

"Marry me," he says into my hair.

I stop pushing him and look at him like he's grown a second head. I can't have heard correctly. No way he just said what I think he did. I shake my head a little and blink. "What?"

"Marry me."

The knock sounds again, harder and more insistent. "Matt, get up. We need to talk," DJ says raspily through the door. Matt looks up and sighs as he lets me go and gets out of bed. He throws a pair of sweats on. I leap out of bed and grab his arm.

"Wait! You can't just ask me to marry you and leave!"

He leans down to kiss me. "I'm not leaving. I'm getting rid of DJ."

The knocking gets louder. "Matt, come on," DJ says almost desperately, but my focus isn't on him or Lyric. It's on the words that just came out of Matt's mouth.

"Forget them. You can't just walk away after asking me to marry you!"

He sighs, then turns towards the dresser. He grabs a little black box and returns to me, dropping to his knee. "I know the idea of an engagement in some fancy place isn't your style. So... Baby. I love you. More than I can even begin to describe. I never believed in love at first sight. Until you. As soon as I saw you, I knew you were it."

The knocking gets harder, but we both ignore it. Matt takes my left hand and kisses it as he flicks the box open and takes out the ring. "I didn't really intend to propose to you while you were naked, but I don't care." He leans forward and kisses my stomach before he looks up at me. "I love you. I love how you are with my family. I love how they all love you. I love how you fit in my life so perfectly. I want to spend the rest of my life with you. Marry me."

I feel a stray tear as I nod my head. "Yes," I whisper. He grins and puts the ring on my finger. He stands, throwing his arms around my waist and lifting me. I wrap my legs and arms around him and he spins me in a circle. "Yes! Yes! Yes!"

He kisses me as the knocking on the door turns to pounding.

"Matt! Mariah! Come on! I'm not fucking around! Answer the damn door, or I'm opening it, and I don't give a shit who I see naked."

"I guess that sounds important." Matt says to me as he looks at me confused and concerned. He puts me down and lets me go. "Get dressed."

He leaves the room, careful in making sure no one sees me, and closes the door behind him. I hurry to get dressed, taking a moment to admire my ring. It's a white gold band with a blue sapphire stone in the middle. On each side of the stone is a butterfly. Each wing holds diamonds and a blue stone. Down each side of the ring, starting at the butterfly, is six small diamonds. It fits me perfectly, and I love everything about it. Especially that it's not huge and gaudy.

I smile as I walk out of the room. The smile immediately drops from my lips. The happiness I felt moments before evaporates as soon as I see the look on Matt's face.

I feel my chest tighten so fast, I have no warning it's going to happen. I fight to breathe. My heart feels like it stops beating. DJ looks at me with the same expression Matt has. A look of pity. Confusion. Distrust.

Of… of resentment. Lyric's face looks somber, and she's hugging herself as she watches me. More pity. More… confusion.

"Mariah, uh…," DJ begins. He looks at me and picks up a stack of papers. "Our Captain intercepted these. We… We're all a close unit. We take care of our own."

He hands me the papers. Matt doesn't look at me. His grip on the counter is white-knuckled. His muscles are straining and bulging. I can see the veins in his arms and his stomach. He looks like he could rip the counter apart if he wanted to.

I look down at the papers in my hand. Restraining order. Filed by my father. Accusations about threats to his life. A gun. I drop the papers to the ground and look at Matt.

"I'm sorry." It's a whisper that I barely hear myself. I don't expect anyone else to. I see Lyric moving towards me, but I'm sure it's just because she feels obligated to. "I'm so sorry."

"Mariah? It's okay. We'll get through this," Lyric whispers into my hair as she wraps her arms around me and hugs me tightly. But her words don't really sink in.

It's over. He's finally done it. My father has succeeded in his goal to ruin my life. It only took him thirty something years.

I should've known. I should've known that things were going too well for me. Falling in love. Following my dreams. Being a published author. Making my own way in life. And actually being good at it. Successful!

How could I think for a single solitary second that I could ever be happy? That any of this could ever be mine? There's no way. No way someone like me could ever find happiness of this level. A love so deep.

"I'm so sorry."

I feel myself slipping into the familiar darkness. The familiar feeling I haven't felt in so many months. The familiar chest tightness. The dizziness. The familiar feeling of not being able to catch my breath. The dark world I fought so hard to come out of.

I sit down on the couch in a daze and look at Matt. I can't hear DJ talking. I barely feel Lyric sit next to me. All I see is Matt. I lost him. I lost everything.

"I'm so, so sorry."

Chapter Twelve

☆ Matt ☆

I grip the counter so hard that I'm pretty sure the marble digging into my hands is making them bleed. That if I let go, blood will be dripping from my palms. I'm glad I don't have my sister's kids right now, and that DJ's son isn't here. That he's staying the night with Beckett at my sister's. They don't need to see me like this.

How the fuck could this happen? How could anyone do something like this to their own daughter? A restraining order. A fucking restraining order based on accusations that don't even make sense. She doesn't talk to him. She doesn't live anywhere near him! She doesn't even own a gun!

I feel a hand on my shoulder and tense.

"Matt," DJ says low and softly.

I look at DJ. I can feel the fire in my eyes, but it gives me some small comfort that it's reflected in his. That he feels as passionately about this as I do.

"How the fuck does this happen?" I ask.

"Matt, it doesn't matter. We can deal with that later." He nods and points to Mariah. "She needs you." She's folded herself into a ball on the couch. Her arms are wrapped around her knees, and her head is tucked between her arms. Lyric has managed to wrap her body around her protectively. I can tell she's speaking softly in her ear.

"Baby," I whisper. Lyric sees me running to her out of the corner of her eye and reluctantly moves out of the way. I sit next to Mariah, pulling her into my lap.

"I'm so sorry," she whispers

"For what?" I hold her tightly to my chest. She's shaking.

"I'm so, so sorry," she whispers into my chest. DJ sits next to me, pulling Lyric into his lap, cuddling her into his chest.

"She kept saying that over and over again. I don't even think she heard a word I said. I think she thinks whatever this is is her fault," Lyric whispers, chewing on her lip.

"It is my fault," Mariah whispers.

"What? Baby, how is this your fault?" I ask.

"I should've known," she says.

"Mariah -"

She cuts me off. "Even DJ said it. They intercepted it. To protect you. Their own. This could ruin your life."

"Mariah," DJ says. "When I said we protect our own, I didn't just mean Matt. I meant you, too."

Mariah looks at me, then him. Lyric reaches out and brushes Mariah's wild hair out of her face. Mariah looks at DJ fearfully and confused. "What?" she asks.

"Yeah, we protect other cops," DJ says. "But also families of cops. To us, you're Matt's wife already. No different than with Lyric and me. Cops protect each other, at least in situations where no harm or wrong-doing is occurring. But we also rally around those that our partners care about. Don't think I missed that ring on your finger. Or that Lyric and I missed him proposing to you. You may just be engaged now, but you're part of our family. Cap intercepted it to protect you."

She looks at me with distress and vulnerability. Lyric leans over and hugs her. I instinctively know I fucked up. "You were so mad. I thought you... hated me," she says over a choked back sob. I hug her tighter to me.

"Mariah, are you joking?" I ask. I know she isn't. I just hate that she could ever think that. That I could cause her to think that.

"I thought when you saw that..." She swallows. Hard.

105

"That I believed it? Baby, I know better than that. We all do. We know his games; his tricks."

"You mean… you believe me?" She hesitantly looks over at DJ and Lyric. "That all of you do?"

"What the hell? Why wouldn't I? I love you, honey." I kiss her cheek and run my fingers through her hair.

"You still love me? Even though my dad is trying to ruin me?"

"Mariah. Sweetheart, I'm never leaving you to fight your battles alone. I know you've had to do that your entire life, but not anymore. You have me. You have Lyric. You have DJ."

"Hell, you have the entire Gainesville Police Department," DJ says as he squeezes her leg. "Ever since that shit with your dad happened last month, Cap flagged your name and his. Anytime your name or his comes up, he gets notified. He got a copy of the order filed when your name came across his desk. He pulled some strings with the Sheriff's Department and said he'd serve you himself. They were emailed a copy of this not long after it was filed."

"Honey, I'm sorry I scared you. I realize that my reaction to that probably looked far different than I thought it did. I'm mad that he's doing this to you. I'm angry at how far you've come over the past year only to have this dropped on you. And I'm even more pissed off that he honestly thinks he can get away with it."

"He's not going to get away with it," Lyric says.

"He says in here that you call him and threaten him. Have you talked to your dad at all since the day of my girl's party after he was released from the psych hold? Other than when he showed up at your apartment?" DJ asks, even though he knows the answer.

"I talked to him the day the police took him for a psych hold because Officer Howard asked me if I could talk him down. And then he called me a couple days later when we were at your daughter's party the day Lyric finally got here. I'm so happy she came early," Mariah whispers as she closes her eyes.

"He yelled at you about how the police showing up at his house and him losing his dog was your fault. You hung up on him," I say. DJ nods. He and Lyric were standing right there just like I was when it happened.

"He's called me since then, but I never picked up. And then the day he showed up at my apartment. But I didn't really talk to him. I was too scared. Matt blocked his number the last time he called before he showed up that day, but he's left me voicemails," she says quietly.

"We've been locking the messages on her phone, though. Just in case he decided to pull some stupid shit like this," I say.

"Smart. I can pull the call records for the past year. It'll show incoming and outgoing calls. Just need your permission to bypass the need for a warrant," DJ says.

"You have her permission," I say for her.

"How do we even know what to do with this?" Lyric asks. "She's not even in Minnesota. She hasn't been for over a year now."

"That's part of our case," I say. "Mariah isn't there. He accused her of kidnapping his dog in that restraining order, but she wasn't there."

"He accused you of threatening him with a gun." DJ grabs the paperwork and looks through it. "Threatening him on January eighth in a phone call. Also February sixth, March twentieth, and April tenth."

"Phone records will prove otherwise," I say. I hug Mariah tighter to me and feel her fear melt away.

"What about the day he said I kidnapped his dog? Or the days he said I threatened him with a gun?"

DJ flips through the papers. "He said the dog kidnapping happened during the time he would've been in the psych hold."

"Officer Howard said they took him to the pound because no one would take him," I say. "As for the gun shit, you were here. You have witnesses. Lyric moved here a couple of days after all of this occurred. So you have all three of us as well as some of the officers in the department."

Mariah grips my shirt, and I run my fingers through her hair. I can sense she's trying to ground herself. DJ and Lyric know her well enough to sense it also.

He reaches out and squeezes her calf. "Hey," DJ says. "We'll take care of this."

Lyric squeezes her hand. "You aren't alone. You've got an entire fucking army with you on this."

DJ nods in agreement. "We can call in Officer Howard to testify you weren't there for the dog kidnapping. You have Matt and I to testify that you were here for everything else. Lyric can testify to everything she

107

was here for if we need her to. She was talking to you all day the day your dad was taken in."

"And I've been here for a lot of those dates, too," Lyric tells her.

She's quiet a few moments. "I'm going to have to fly to Duluth… aren't I?"

I sigh and hug her a little tighter. "It's for the best, honey."

"But Matt will fly up there with you, Mariah. And so will me and Lyric. We've seen the attacks your dad causes. We've been there for a few of them. I think Lyric has been there in some way for all of them. We can give the Judge the evidence we have that he's lying, and we can testify in person that all of this is bullshit. We can testify to your reaction to him every time he calls or we talk about him."

"The point is you aren't doing this alone," Lyric offers.

"Actually I think we need to file a counter restraining order against him," I say. "The harassment order we got might have deterred him for a little while, but now he's using the courts. He came here to Gainesville and threatened her. We can use that, even though she didn't want to at first."

"Not a bad idea," DJ agrees.

"She feared for her life and yours. All of ours. She told us," Lyric says.

"I can get Duluth to fax paperwork while I'm pulling phone records," DJ puts in. "We can get everything together when I get home. I'll go now."

I rub Mariah's arm and tug her hair a little so she looks at me. "What do you think?"

"Honestly? That I'm scared."

I kiss her softly. "I know you are. But you don't need to be. We'll deal with this together, baby."

She nods and hugs me.

"You're not doing this alone," Lyric says.

"You'll never be alone again, Mariah. Not as long as I have a say in it," I tell her.

"Or me," DJ says.

"Or me," Lyric chips in.

We all lean in and engulf Mariah in a group hug until we feel her relax. I catch DJ's eye and know we need to figure this out. I don't want

Mariah getting more and more worked up while we go through paperwork and work out details.

"Mariah? Why don't you and Lyric start talking about the wedding? DJ and I will deal with everything else. Take some time to come down. By the time we're done, you'll feel better. Sound good?"

She nods against my chest. We all slowly release her. Lyric curls up with her on the couch while DJ and I stand, walking to another room as I keep an eye on her. There's squealing as they both admire her ring. Before long, they're browsing the internet, our upcoming nuptials surprisingly providing the perfect distraction.

"This entire restraining order is bullshit, Matt," DJ says, effectively wiping the soft smile Mariah put on my face off of it.

I look down at it. "Yeah. I know." I shake my head. "He says she kidnapped his dog. He fears she killed him. She was standing outside his house at night with a rifle. Several nights. She called him and threatened him. He found a shell casing for an AR-15 where she was standing. What is this?" I shake my head, incredulous.

DJ looks down at it. "He said she broke into his house with the police and tried to get him committed."

"But these are the dates that he was here."

DJ shrugs. "You know as well as I do he's had time for the paranoia to set in. Gives him a fuck of a lot of time to work himself up and spin everything that happened, everything he thinks he saw, into whatever the fuck this is." He gestures to the restraining order.

"We need to file a counter. We have no choice. I know Mariah doesn't want to, but there isn't an option here."

"We need to counter all of this first."

"That's what you're going to be doing when you get her phone records. We need to figure out what to put in the counter order against him. I had intended to let all of that go like she wanted me to. I thought a harassment order would be enough, even though she didn't want me to bother with that either, but fuck it. I don't want him to come anywhere near her. I have no doubt he'll retaliate after getting this bullshit thrown out of court."

"Him showing up the way he did should be enough."

"We can add the harassment into it. All the phone calls. All the dates. We can do that with those phone records." I start writing everything down. "We need to prove she was terrified for her life."

"Shouldn't be hard. When we got there, she was frozen. Lyric was trying fucking hard to get to her, but there was no way in hell I was letting her go. I didn't know if he had weapons or what the fuck was going on."

"Fuck, I didn't know if he had weapons. I was just trying to keep him from getting to her."

"She was terrified. She couldn't move. She was afraid he was going to hurt all of us. He traveled fifteen hundred fucking miles to fuck with her, Matt."

"Well, we'll have her testimony to that. We'll have ours. We can add all of that into it and list me, you, Lyric, and Brody as witnesses to her state of mind and reaction to him."

I let out a long breath as we continue making a list of everything that we need to address. The phone calls. Him showing up here. Everything that he put in his restraining order that we need to counter. I refuse to let him fuck with my girl. She's worked harder than anyone I've ever seen to get as far as she has. I won't let him and his psychotic antics set her back on the progress she's made.

I glance up at her sweet giggle and smile softly as I watch her and Lyric planning our future. Seeing her come out of the sadness and mild panic she just went through is heartwarming. She needs that sense of calm right now. I'll be thankful to Lyric every day for the rest of my life that she knows how to be the distraction that relaxes my girl when I can't be.

Despite everything going on with Mariah's dad, the most important thing to me is that she said 'yes.' She agreed to be my partner for the rest of our lives. When it comes down to it, the only thing that matters to me is her. And I'd do anything to keep that beautiful smile on her perfect face.

Chapter Thirteen

☆ Mariah ☆

I left Duluth to get away from everything and everyone. I left so I could start my own life. Live my own life. I left to get away from the constant criticism from people who refused to support me. I left to get away from my father. From him leaning on me because no one else was there for him. I left to get away from him blaming me for everything that happened to him when he was off his meds.

When I was around him, I was constantly on guard. Walking on eggshells. Making sure nothing I said or did would set him off. I had to bite my tongue, more than once, just to keep the peace. In the end, he was one of the reasons I had to leave. He was a large contribution to the damage being done to my health and well-being. The stress he put on me was overwhelming. Just being near him sent my anxiety into instant overdrive.

Lyric puts her hand on my back and leans over to hug me. "Are you okay?"

I sigh and shake my head, leaning into her. "Not really. But I'm trying. He's not here yet. Court starts in a few minutes." I glance towards the elevators when I hear a chime. Every chime I hear makes my heart beat faster.

"Maybe he won't show."

I watch as my dad walks off the elevator. He makes eye contact with me. I shrink into myself. "No such luck."

"You'll be okay. You have Matt and DJ with you. And me. You're not alone."

I watch as my dad speaks in hushed tones to a Bailiff. After a few moments, the Bailiff walks towards us. "Ms. Carter. I'm going to have to ask that you come with me," the Bailiff says.

"What? Why?" I ask, nearing the stages of a complete freak out.

"You're breaking a restraining order. You can't be here," he says to me as he starts taking out his cuffs. I nearly stop breathing and look at Matt and DJ, quickly passing the stages of nearing panic and actually reaching it in record time. DJ puts an arm around me, tugging me protectively into his side. Lyric presses herself against my side, narrowing her eyes at the Bailiff with a low growl before turning her glare on my dad, as Matt stands to deal with him.

"Hang on. She's here because the hearing for the restraining order is today," Matt says.

"The restraining order has already been granted. Mr. Peterson is here on a different matter and informed me that you're here to intimidate him," the Bailiff says to me, ignoring Matt as he starts to move for my arm to drag me up. I cling to DJ as Lyric tightens her grip on me as she moves to shield me. I try to fight back my attack. I don't want to show my father his effect on me, but it's getting harder the more I'm threatened with an arrest.

"I don't know what he told you, but the hearing is today, and she has every right to be here for that. She has a right to defend herself against the accusations he's made," DJ says. DJ pulls out the restraining order, fighting against my grip on his arm. He shows the Bailiff the date for the hearing.

"She's not doing anything wrong," Matt says. "She's showing up at court to contest the restraining order and file one of her own. You can't stop her from doing that."

I look up at Matt, tears stinging my eyes as I whisper. "Matt?"

112

"Don't worry, baby," Matt says. "He's just trying to manipulate the situation." He's glaring at the Bailiff.

The Bailiff hands DJ back the papers and nods. "Sorry for this misunderstanding. Thanks for clearing that up." The Bailiff looks pissed as he walks away. I'm shaking. Lyric is hugging me tightly while DJ is trying to shield me. Matt puts his arm around me and hugs me close to his chest. I refuse to let go of DJ or Lyric, so the hug turns into a group hug.

"Did he seriously just try to get her arrested?" DJ asks.

"He didn't think she'd show up to defend herself," Matt says.

"Peterson versus Carter. Right this way please," the Bailiff says.

Matt and DJ stand. Lyric pulls me up with her. DJ and Matt shield us both as my dad walks in. After a moment, they guide us into the courtroom.

"I'm so scared, Matt," I whisper.

"I know, baby. I'm right here. I'll sit between you and him," Matt says. I feel DJ's hand on the small of my back as he guides me to the chair next to Matt in the front of the courtroom.

"And I'll be right here on the other side, sweetheart. Lyric is right behind you. He won't get to you," DJ says. I take a deep breath as I sit. The hearing gets underway. I glance back at Lyric, and she gives me a reassuring nod, reaching out to gently squeeze my shoulder. She keeps her hand there to help ground me. To remind me she's there.

"Mr. Peterson," the Judge begins. "It looks like you've filed a restraining order against Ms. Carter because of threats and violent tendencies against you and..." He looks down at the paperwork in front of him. "Your dog."

"Yes, Judge. She's made several threats over the phone and in person," my father says.

"We'll get to that in a moment," the Judge says. "Ms. Carter. You're filing a counter restraining and renewal on your expired harassment order against Mr. Peterson."

I try to look up, but I fail. I swallow. "Yes, sir." I try to talk louder, but I can't. My chest feels like it's going to collapse. I wipe away a tear.

I feel Lyric gently squeeze my shoulder again, whispering to me. "You've got this, honey."

"And who is it you've brought with you today?" the Judge asks.

"U-um..." I try to swallow the panic. I look at Matt and try to focus on him, but I can see my dad watching me. Matt stands and DJ puts a hand on my leg as tears sting my eyes. I can feel Lyric's hand on my shoulder, and it helps keep me together.

"Your Honor, my name is Matt Chance. I'm a Sergeant with the Gainesville Police Department in Florida. Next to Ms. Carter is DJ Rens. He is also a Sergeant with the Gainesville Police Department. We also have a few officers here with the Duluth Police Department who are here to testify on behalf of Ms. Carter regarding the accusations Mr. Peterson made in his restraining order. We also have a close friend who has witnessed just as much, if not more, than Sergeant Rens and I have in regards to these accusations. Regarding the fight Mr. Peterson is speaking of, we have another witness here to testify to that."

"Very well. Ms. Carter, you look terrified," the Judge says. "I must tell you, you are perfectly safe in my courtroom, but I'm assuming you'd like Sergeant Chance and Sergeant Rens to remain with you?"

I nod my head. "Yes, Your Honor. Please."

"Very well," the Judge says. "Mr. Peterson. Let's begin, please."

"Thank you," my father begins. "About a year ago, I was working with the Duluth Police Department to solve a rash of unsolved murders. I found out that my downstairs neighbor was involved, and I informed my contact. He said he would investigate it and take care of it. I suspected that he was in on it. After he didn't come to arrest the downstairs person, I contacted the department to file a complaint on him and to tell them that if they didn't come, I would take care of the problem on my own."

"Mr. Peterson," the Judge says. "This has nothing to do with Ms. Carter or your restraining order."

"I'm getting to that."

"Please. Do that."

"My daughter, Ms. Carter, sent the entire department. All of her contacts. She called me several times to tell me that they were going to kill me to shut me up."

My mouth drops open. I look at Matt. Tears begin to fall from my eyes as I whisper to him. "I never said that. I didn't do that."

Matt squeezes the hand that he'd been holding underneath the table and DJ rubs the leg that he hasn't let go of since we sat down. I turn to Lyric. She gives me a nod and smiles, but I can see the inferno behind her hazel eyes. I'll never be more grateful for the three people I have with me today. They'll never understand the extent of my gratitude.

Matt looks at me and whispers, "Shh... We know. We'll get our chance."

"It broke my heart to find out my daughter was involved, and the only way to survive was to go to the hospital. But when I got released, she called me and threatened me more. She said she killed my dog and would kill me next. I saw her across the street from my house with a rifle. Police issued." He reaches into his coat pocket and pulls out a plastic baggie. "I found these where she was standing. One of them is spent."

"Live ammunition?" DJ whispers in disbelief. Matt looks horrified as he shields my body with his. DJ immediately moves behind me to shield Lyric.

"What is that?" she whispers, frightened.

"Shh. It's okay, beautiful. I've got you. You're safe," DJ whispers back to her. I'm too terrified to look back and see if she's okay.

"Mr. Peterson!" the Judge nearly yells. "You can't just bring live ammunition into my courtroom. Bailiff, get that away from him!"

"Do I get that back?" my father asks.

"Absolutely not!" the Judge says.

"You can't keep my evidence!" my father yells.

"Continue with your presentation, Mr. Peterson, or you'll be held in contempt!" the Judge yells right back.

I can't breathe. My chest isn't even moving anymore. It hurts to take a breath. "I... I have to get out of here." I stand to leave, but Matt grabs my arm. DJ puts his hand on my shoulder, keeping me firmly in my chair.

"He won't hurt you, honey. I promise," Matt whispers. I stay, but I'm shaking. I clasp my hands in my lap and look straight ahead. I can't stop the tears that fall silently. DJ sits next to me again but turns so he can see Lyric. I feel her place her hand comfortingly back on my shoulder.

"I saw her there twice. Both times at night. She called me several times threatening me. I've hardly even left my house. She has her contacts following me everywhere. I just want to live a normal life without her harassing me and threatening me."

The Judge looks back at the papers in front of him. "It says here that she tried to get you thrown into a psychiatric facility, and had two of her contacts beat you up."

"She came to my house and broke in. The two people she had with her are police officers. I found out they're Duluth Police Officers posing as the Gainesville officers you see here today."

DJ chuckles quietly and shakes his head. I hear Lyric growl under her breath behind me. I don't even need to look to know she has a fierce glare aimed at him. I can't believe the lies coming out of his mouth. I feel like an unprepared little girl trying to fight an invisible enemy. An enemy that I can't see coming no matter how hard I prepare because his strategy is unpredictable.

The Judge sighs. I can't tell if he believes my father's lies or not. "Ms. Carter, I expect you are planning to counter?"

"Yes, Your Honor." But I don't know how. I can barely speak. I take a deep, shaky breath and reach for the papers in front of Matt as I stand. "Um..." I don't even know where to begin. I can't even hold my hands steady. DJ clears his throat and stands, putting a hand over mine to steady me.

"Your Honor, Ms. Carter suffers from severe anxiety," DJ begins. "Being around her father is actually causing a panic attack right now that she's trying really hard to fight, even though you can clearly see it."

"She can answer your questions, Your Honor, but presenting this is something she's really struggling with while Mr. Peterson is in the same room," Matt says as he also stands.

"We understand that Mr. Peterson has the right to hear accusations against him, but would there be a problem with Sergeant Chance and I presenting to you on Ms. Carter's behalf?" DJ asks.

The Judge looks at the three of us a moment as he thinks. "This is unorthodox. Ms. Carter, if I have questions, you'll need to answer them. Can you do that?"

I give him a shaky nod. My stomach starts clenching. "Yes, Your Honor."

"Very well. Then you may proceed," the Judge agrees. I sit down.

Matt glances at the papers. "To begin, we have Officer Howard here from the Duluth Police Department. If it's okay with you, we'd like him to begin with information regarding what happened the day Mr. Peterson said Ms. Carter sent her contacts after him to keep him quiet."

"We think it would be more beneficial for you to hear what happened from the police department's point of view before Ms. Carter's," DJ says.

"Okay. Officer Howard. You may step forward," the Judge says. Officer Howard steps forward and stands next to Matt. He gives me a soft smile.

"Your Honor," Officer Howard says. "On September twenty-sixth, we received a phone call from Mr. Peterson regarding his downstairs neighbor. He told us his neighbor was involved in several murders in the area. We'd received many calls from him during the month of September. He was reporting murders, and telling us where the bodies were. I had taken several of the calls myself. I believe you have the reports."

"I do," the Judge says.

"We knew his mental health history because nearly every time he called, an officer contacted Ms. Carter. She'd tell us. On September twenty sixth, I contacted her because he had barricaded himself in his house. I thought that maybe she'd be able to help talk him out. I set up a three way call with her. I had Ms. Carter call him, then patch me in."

"So you were involved in this call that Mr. Peterson believes was threatening?" the Judge asks.

"Yes, Your Honor. But it was anything but. In fact, it was Mr. Peterson threatening her. Ms. Carter actually ended the call after Mr. Peterson told her that he had planned to take care of her and all of her contacts. And that was only after Ms. Carter had spent nearly two hours on the phone with him trying to talk him out. He had threatened her several times up until that point. We do have the call recorded via my body camera. I had my squad's cell phone on speaker. I believe you also have the call as well as the transcripts from it."

"You can't record someone in the State of Minnesota without their consent," my father says condescendingly.

"That doesn't apply to body camera footage, Mr. Peterson," the Judge says. I can tell he's getting annoyed.

"We were able to get him out much later that night," Officer Howard continues. "We had been there for ten hours. Mr. Peterson was ultimately taken to the hospital where he was held in a seventy-two hour psychiatric hold."

"Thank you, Officer Howard," the Judge says. "You may be seated. Are the other two officers here to testify about that day as well, Sergeant Chance?"

"The Duluth officers are here to testify about that day and the days leading up to it, Your Honor," Matt answers.

"I don't need to hear anymore on that subject. I have the necessary information," the Judge says as he starts reading what I think is probably the transcript from the phone call. At least enough to corroborate what Officer Howard said.

"We have Lyric Sharpe here today, as well," DJ says. "During the day Mr. Peterson was in a standoff with the police, Ms. Carter's anxiety started to take hold because of all the phone calls she was getting and because of the entire situation. She's here to testify to exactly the state Mariah was in as a direct result of being contacted all day."

The Judge motions Lyric forward. I want to turn around, but I physically can't. I can't turn to look at her when she gets up near the table because if I do, I'll see my father. DJ stands and moves behind me, closer to Lyric. Out of the corner of my eye, I see her shoot my father a withering glare.

Her strength.

I wish I had her strength.

"Ms. Sharpe, were you there during the phone calls from the police?" the Judge asks.

"No, sir. At the time I lived in the United Kingdom. I was talking to Mariah via text message and Instagram chat as well as Skype. She was really upset. She told me everything that was happening. Eventually, though, she stopped talking all together. I couldn't get ahold of her. So I called my boyfriend in hopes he could get ahold of her boyfriend since they work together with the Gainesville Police Department."

"Is her boyfriend here?" the Judge asks, looking around the room.

"I'm her boyfriend, Your Honor," Matt answers.

"My boyfriend is Sergeant DJ Rens." She gestures to DJ. "He couldn't get ahold of Matt because Matt was on a call," Lyric continues. "As soon as Mariah stopped responding to me, I became worried. After a couple of hours of not being able to get ahold of her in any way, I called

DJ and told him what was happening. He immediately headed for Mariah's apartment complex and waited until Matt cleared the call he was on, as he didn't want Matt to become worried and be put in more danger on the call than he already was as the responding officer. As soon as Matt cleared, DJ contacted him. I was still on the phone with DJ when he got to the apartment. Mariah was nearly catatonic. DJ couldn't get her to talk. When Matt arrived, Mariah still hadn't said a word. I was able to work with them to get Mariah to calm down. To respond to us. It was clear, even through the phone, that she was terrified."

"Ms. Carter was having a panic attack?" the Judge asks.

"Yes, Your Honor. I'd been able to talk her down from several of them over the course of our friendship and even that day. But every time the Duluth Police called her that day, her attacks got worse. By the time I called DJ, I was so scared about her state and that I couldn't get ahold of her... I just knew instinctively that she needed help. So I got it for her. When she started to respond, even though she was terrified, she was still worried about her dad. Her first reaction when she started to come out of the catatonic state was that she had to get to Duluth. She had to help him. She didn't want him to get hurt. We talked her down. Then Matt spoke to the officer who was on the phone while DJ and I continued to keep her calm. Matt took control of the situation as he didn't want her to go into another panic attack."

"Thank you Ms. Sharpe. You may be seated." Lyric shoots me a confident smile and leans over the railing, squeezing my shoulder as she sits in her seat behind me. "Sergeant Chance, it looks like you'd like to contest her whereabouts during and after Mr. Peterson's confinement, and you also have phone records."

"Your Honor, we have phone records for each date that Mr. Peterson stated Ms. Carter contacted him." DJ hands the stack of papers to the Bailiff. "We'd like to counter the portion in Mr. Peterson's restraining order regarding the phone calls he said she made threatening him. Highlighted are the phone calls made on the days Mr. Peterson highlights. You'll also see the phone calls received," DJ says.

"You'll see that Mr. Peterson actually contacted her on those dates, and that the phone calls were short," Matt jumps in.

119

"This is because Ms. Carter never answered. Mr. Peterson left messages. We have those messages locked on Ms. Carter's phone if you'd like to listen to them," DJ continues.

"Yes, please," the Judge says, holding out his hand. Matt hands the Bailiff my phone. The Judge listens to each message, putting the phone on speaker. I watch his face grow more and more angry.

"Those calls are faked!" my dad bursts out.

"Quiet!" the Judge demands. After he's done, he hands the phone to the Bailiff. The Bailiff hands it to Matt.

"On September thirtieth, there's a phone call that lasts thirteen minutes," the Judge says.

"Yes, Your Honor. Mr. Peterson contacted Ms. Carter after he was released from the hold," Matt responds.

"What was discussed, Ms. Carter?" the Judge asks, looking directly at me. I look up at Matt. He smiles and nods. I clear my throat. I look back at Lyric, willing some of her strength to rub off on me. She's sitting there like a warrior. She gives me a reassuring look. I don't stand. I'm far too scared to do something stupid like that.

"Um... It started civil enough. I asked... how he was. If he had gotten everything regulated with his medication... If he felt better. He said he felt better, but then he started yelling at me."

"Sergeant Rens and I saw the expression on her face. We both quickly made our way to her, taking her into a private room. Lyric saw what was happening and followed us. DJ and I had Mariah put it on speaker," Matt says.

"The three of you were there?" the Judge asks.

"Yes, Your Honor," DJ says. "It was my son's birthday. Sergeant Chance and Ms. Carter brought Sergeant Chance's nieces and nephew. Lyric had just moved here. She had just arrived that morning."

"Ms. Carter. What was your father yelling about?"

"Um... That he knew I kidnapped his dog. He said I killed him... His dog. He said that he saw me in front of his house that morning with a gun. In the paperwork he said at night, but on the phone he said that morning. I told him that I was in Florida. That it wasn't possible for me to have been there."

"You were in Florida?" the Judge asks.

"I live in Florida, Your Honor. At that time, I'd been there just over a month."

"So I'm guessing there's an alibi for the other dates he said he saw you," the Judge says, chuckling.

"Your Honor," DJ says. "She hasn't left Florida since she moved."

"I've been with her at some point every single day since I helped her move in. DJ has spoken with her on the phone or been with her most every single day since that day. He also helped her move in. And Lyric has been with her at some point every day since she moved to the United States," Matt says.

"With all due respect, I left Minnesota for several reasons, Your Honor." I take a deep breath, willing my voice and hands to stop shaking. It doesn't work, but I know I need to get this out. "One of them is my father. I had no intention of ever coming back here. Ever. The only reason I'm here right now is because I was convinced doing this in person instead of a video hearing was the best idea." I wipe away another stubborn tear.

The Judge nods. "The last matter here is regarding a break-in to his house. I see in your counter restraining order, the same day he says you broke into his house, you say he came to your apartment in Gainesville. You have police reports and another witness from the Gainesville Police Department."

"Yes, Your Honor," I whisper.

"Okay," the Judge begins. "I've heard enough on both matters. I don't need to hear any more testimony. I have the police reports right here. Mr. Peterson. I'm not granting you your restraining order. It's obvious to me that nothing you brought here is true. I would charge you with perjury, but I honestly believe that you believe everything you said is the truth because of your mental state. That being said. Ms. Carter. I am granting you your restraining and harassment order request. Mr. Peterson, you are not allowed to contact Ms. Carter in any form. Phone, email, or social media for a period of one year. You are also not allowed within five hundred feet of her or her residence."

I feel like a giant weight has been lifted off my shoulders as I sink into my seat. DJ and Matt both hug me, and I feel Lyric's hand on my shoulder in both support and comfort.

"After a period of one year, this matter can be revisited, and the order can be extended if needed. That's my ruling. Case dismissed."

"Oh my God," I whisper. So much relief passes through me that I nearly collapse when I try to stand on my feet.

"Ms. Carter, I'll keep Mr. Peterson here while you leave the courtroom. I apologize again about earlier," the Bailiff says.

I smile as Matt leads me out of the courtroom. DJ and Lyric follow. When we walk outside, I take a deep, calming, refreshing breath, as Matt, DJ, and Lyric all surround me, hugging me firmly.

Finally. Finally, I'm free of him.

Epilogue

☆ Matt ☆

(One Year Later)

I grin like a fool as my two nieces walk down the aisle throwing flowers. In a few moments my life is about to begin. I'd been happy before. I loved my life. My family. My job. But I never realized for a second that my life wasn't anywhere near complete.

Not until Mariah walked into it.

Brit and Marie are both wearing dark pink halter style dresses. Their hair is down. They are wearing a crown of pink carnations with baby's breath in their hair. They're throwing pink carnation petals for Mariah to walk over as she makes her way to me.

"She's coming, Uncle Matt," Brit says as she reaches me.

"And she looks so pretty," Marie breathes in a whisper as she also reaches me. I smile as I lean down to hug them.

"I bet she does," I whisper to them. They scurry over to Elizabeth and Beckett, who is sitting next to Layne, DJ's son, and sit down. I stand and glance at Lyric, giving her a smile as she beams up the aisle. She's wearing a pink halter style dress that matches the girls and hits just below her knee. She also wears a crown of carnations and baby's breath in her hair. The breeze coming off the Atlantic Ocean gently blows the skirt of her dress around her legs.

Mariah and I were both ecstatic that Lyric decided to move to the United States earlier than she'd planned. We both believe we have DJ to thank for a lot of it. Though, I don't think there was any chance Lyric would have been able to stay away, especially after what happened with Mariah.

I couldn't believe how happy Lyric and Mariah were when the decision to move earlier than planned had been made. The two had been close as they could be since they met, but now that they are in the same country? May the State of Florida be able to contain the two.

As the music starts for Mariah, I glance at DJ standing next to me. He tears his eyes away from Lyric long enough to look up the aisle as Mariah appears.

Mariah had opened up quite a bit since I met her two years ago. She got along great with my family. Putting herself out there to make friends was something she was working on but still struggled with.

I was grateful as hell that she and DJ had hit it off. Ever since they met when he helped me help her move in, he's become one of her two best friends.

DJ smiles at me and winks. We had decided on white tuxes since we are getting married on the beach. His tux matches mine right down to the pink tie that matches the girl's dresses. The only difference is the dark pink carnation I have pinned to my lapel. My girl hates traditional flowers, but give her a carnation, and she'll do anything for you.

We both grin as the audience stands. Mariah appears at the end of the aisle on the arm of my Captain. After we got back from Duluth, Captain Brody McKay, had taken a serious interest in being around Mariah. Truth is, he likes her, and he always wanted a daughter. He has two sons.

He started out being like a mentor to her, but after he started checking in on her every day, the mentorship turned into something far more. He was like the father my girl never had or even dared to want.

Mariah meets my eyes as Cap escorts her down the aisle. After our eyes are locked, we don't look away from each other. Her dress is a spaghetti strap, sweetheart neckline that shows off every part of her that I love looking at. Her pure white dress is long and flowing while still light enough that the breeze can carry it around her ankles. The train drags across the aisle, but it doesn't look like it's too heavy for my petite girl.

She's beautiful. Her long dark hair is down, and she has a crown of pink carnations and baby's breath in her hair that matches the girls and Lyric. She's so incredibly beautiful that I can't believe she's mine. I can't believe she wants me. Of all of the men in the world that she could have, this perfect, beautiful woman in front of me chose *me*.

"Matt," Cap says to me. "You are lucky as hell she fell in your lap. Our laps. Hell. We're all lucky to have met this girl." I smile as he hugs Mariah close to him and shakes my hand. "Take care of each other."

"Yes, sir," I say. He puts her hand in mine. I pull her close to me.

"I feel like I've waited my entire life for you," she whispers. I can't resist. I lean down to brush my lips across hers.

"I love you," I whisper against her lips.

"I love you, too."

"Looks like you two are already ready to get this done," the Officiant jokes.

Everyone around us laughs, but I barely hear anything the officiant says as he begins the ceremony. I'm lost in Mariah's eyes. I live for her smile. For the sun's golden rays dancing brilliant colors across her hair. I live for her.

"Matt," the Officiant's voice cuts through my thoughts. "If you'll recite your vows please."

I brush Mariah's hair behind her ear and hold her cheek in my palm. "Mariah. I love you. When I first saw you pulled over on the side of the road crying your eyes out, I knew. I knew I wanted to get to know you. And the more I got to know you, the more time I wanted to spend with you. I wanted to be the one to take care of you. I wanted to be your Captain America." I drop my hand and take both of hers. "I'm so lucky you let me. I'm lucky you love my family as much as I do. I'm lucky you let me in and trusted me with your heart. I'll never break it. I'll always be here for you. I won't love you for the rest of your life, baby. I'll love you for the rest of mine."

"Matt..." I reach up and wipe a tear away from her eye.

"And Mariah," the Officiant says. "Your vows?"

She smiles as she takes my hands in hers. "Matt. I think I loved you the moment I saw you. Even though I didn't want to. I wanted to just start my life over. Alone. I never expected you. I never expected that you would accept me with all of my crazy and love me as much as I know you do. I didn't expect you to stick by me when my life started to fall apart. I didn't expect you to hold me up through all of it. I didn't expect to fall in love with you. But I love this. All of this. I can't envision my life without you. You're everything I've ever wanted but didn't know I needed. I love you. So much."

"May we have the rings?" the Officiant asks. DJ hands me our wedding bands, and I give Mariah mine. We each slide our rings on each other's finger. We take each other's hands.

"Rings represent eternal love," the Officiant begins. "A sacred bond that can never be broken. The rings exchanged between the two of you are a symbolic example of a bond of love between you. With these rings, your love and commitment to each other is sealed in front of all of these witnesses and God."

I squeeze Mariah's hand. She smiles.

"Please…," the Officiant says, "Repeat after me. With these rings we commit to love, honor, and protect each other."

We repeat the words as we look at each other.

"By the power given to me by the State of Florida, I now pronounce you husband and wife. Matt. You may kiss your bride."

I don't hesitate. I pull her close and kiss her like I need her to breathe. And I do. She's more important to me than air.

She brushes her fingers across my face, then around the back of my neck. She pulls me into her and deepens the kiss. Our family and friends fill our ears with hoots and hollers. Brit and Marie laugh hysterically. Beckett whistles.

Finally, we break apart from each other. I take her hand, leading her up the aisle as our friends and family applaud.

"Ready to do this, Mrs. Chance?" I ask as I squeeze her hand.

She squeezes my hand back. "More than ever, Mr. Chance."

I grin down at my girl. My beautiful, strong as hell girl. My love. My life.

"You know," Mariah says as she looks me up and down. "I always thought you looked great in your uniform, but I really like you in that tux."

I laugh as I smile down at her. I kiss her as we head to the reception.

Lyric and Mariah hug each other and laugh as they walk to the head table. The girls waste no time running for that dance floor and goofily dancing to some techno dance jam. They laugh as they spin each other around the dance floor. They find Beckett and Layne and pull them both onto the dance floor with them. Before long, the boys let loose and are spinning the girls in circles.

"Go, Beckett and Layne!" Both Lyric and Mariah call out to him, watching with bright smiles.

Beckett and Layne hear them as wicked grins plaster their faces. They both whisper to the girls, and the four of them run to the head table and drag Mariah and Lyric onto the dance floor with them. They all laugh like they don't have a care in the world as DJ and I hang back and watch.

"You're pretty lucky she gave you a chance," DJ says as he lightly jabs my side.

I smile. "I didn't really give her a choice. I'm lucky she chose to move here, though. I can't imagine my life without her."

"None of us can," he says.

"Without her, you wouldn't have met Lyric. She's perfect for you."

DJ smiles softly as he watches his girl. "I'm proposing."

I look over at him, slightly astounded. "Really? You? I mean, I know things are going well, but I guess I thought you'd want to wait a little while."

"Lyric is my whole life. I fell hard and fucking fast for that girl. She's everything I didn't know I wanted or needed. To put it in the words you and Mariah are always using. I don't want to wait anymore. I know what I want. I know it's her."

"You do complement each other pretty well. That girl may be tiny compared to you, but fuck if she takes any of your shit." I give him a teasing grin.

He laughs. "Lyric is an amazing woman. She's unlike anyone I've ever been with. And you're right. She puts me in my place like no one else. Truth be told, she's a strong as hell woman, but she appeals to my dominant side on all levels. Even if she can be a bit of a brat at times."

"Not just the bedroom?" I wink and elbow his side.

He elbows me back. "Asshole. No. Not just the bedroom."

"I'm only teasing. I'm glad you found her."

"I'm glad Mariah brought her into my life."

"So? What about this proposal?"

DJ smiles. "She loves books. I'm going to take her to the New York Public Library."

"Knowing Lyric, you'd better propose outside. As soon as you get her inside, you'll never find her."

"Sure I would. If they have a romance section, that's where she'll be."

We both laugh as we walk to the head table and take our seats. Mariah smiles up at me as she and Lyric take their seats, both slightly winded from the dance floor extravaganza. I lean down to kiss her.

This.

I'll never need anything more than what I have right now.

She made my life perfect.

Whole.

Complete.

The End

Next In The Beautiful Dream Series

The sweet and sinfully sexy Beautiful Dream Series continues with *My Love, My Heart*!

My relationship with my favorite author, Mariah Marie, started with a message telling her I love her books. She actually messaged me back and made my entire day. We talked every day from then on, and our relationship blossomed into this explosion of passionate fire.

I've always been willing to do anything for love. Even if it means leaving everything I know behind.

We couldn't be happier.

Everything changes the day Mariah comes home terrified.

She's shaken to her core. I've never seen my girl so terrified. I feel like I'm out of my depth, and I'm forced to get help. Problem is, I don't know anyone except our sexy, tattooed neighbor, Lieutenant Matt Chance, an incredibly hot cop who Mariah and I are head over heels in love with.

Matt could possibly be the biggest mistake, or the best decision I've ever made. He confesses his feelings and makes a vow to protect us both, no matter the cost.

I'm not sure he realizes the power he holds over me and Mariah. He'll either save us, or destroy us both forever.

Order *My Love, My Heart* Today!

The Beautiful Dream Series

Available Now

Loving You
My Love, My Heart
Softening Lyric
Undercover Temptations
Captain Charming
Breaking Boundaries
Crashing Into You
Tactical Inferno
Ravishing Our Queen
Cherished By The Texan
Unveiling Our Passions

Box Sets Available

The Beautiful Dream Series: Box Set: Part 1
The Beautiful Dream Series: Box Set: Part 2

Other Books By Melony Ann

The Crane Family Series

Available Now

The Reluctant Mafia King
Sweet Lies
Billion Dollar Love Story
Be Mine
Protecting Her
Dangerously Forbidden Love
His Heart
Love In The Dark

Box Sets Available

The Crane Family Series

The Deimos Trilogy

Available Now

Connor's Legacy
Aryan's Alpha
Kade's Redemption

Box Sets Available

The Deimos Trilogy

The Forbidden Temptation Series

Available Now

The Detective's Forbidden Temptation
The Running Back's Forbidden Temptation

The Lucinio Family Series

Available Now

Rising From The Ashes
The Player's Rebel
Encrypting My Heart
Fighting My Fate

Multi Author Series
Piper Falls: Firehouse 49

Available Now

Ignite My Fire by Melony Ann
Regain My Fire by Kindra White
Playing With My Fire by D.L. Howe
Fight My Fire by Darley Collins
Against My Fire by Anneke Boshoff
Relight My Fire by Louise Murchie
Harness My Fire by Ayana Lisbet
Quench My Fire by Havana Wilder

Let's Be Friends

Follow me on

Bookbub

Facebook

Goodreads

Instagram

Tik Tok

Visit my website
www.melonyannauthor.com

Subscribe to my newsletter and get a FREE never-seen-before NOVELLA
just for subscribers!
https://www.melonyannauthor.com/exclusive-content

Join my Facebook Reader Group!
Melony Ann's Sizzling Book Nook
https://www.facebook.com/groups/melonyannssizzlingbooknook

The official Beautiful Dream Series Playlist on YouTube
https://youtube.com/playlist?list=PLGEiD5wbQmDe1z4_FeeKbMLcBkOz
1M4L4

Dedication

You're the moment we were lucky enough to capture. The light to our dark. The hand that always pulls us through.

Acknowledgements

To Lyric... Laura. In this book, you're a friend. In real life, you're so much more. I don't think I could ever put into words the amount of love I have for you. It's so far off the charts, it doesn't even measure in this galaxy. You've managed to open my eyes to a world I didn't know existed. To be a part of it, and to be exploring it with you is... Well, it's truly incredible. I'm so happy you're by my side on this journey.

To DJ... Jay. You'll never understand how amazing you are. And how you had a hand in saving my life. Like Brad and Laura, I love you beyond words. When the original edition of this book was released, you were nothing more than an incredible man I knew who helped me survive lonely nights. Nights that all of those demons were attacking my mind. But you were never just a friend. You've always been more than that in my heart. You're one of the greatest men I've ever had the pleasure of knowing, and I love you so much.

And finally... To Matt - Brad. You seriously came out of nowhere. I've known of you for so long, but we've only really started to get to know each other. I feel like I've known you my entire life, though. You're such an amazing person, and I feel so lucky that out of all the women in the world that you could have, you chose me. I know I'm not a perfect person, but to you I am. I love you. Thank you for being here for me, and for loving me as much as I love you.

Anneke – You're an angel. Sometimes, I have to question where you tuck your wings.

Jason - It seems to not matter the time that passes or the distance. You mean the world.

Kayla - I'm so happy to have gotten to know you. You're just a beautiful soul.

To the Bookstagram Community.

To my family.

To all of those who believe in me and support me.

To all of those who don't.

Cover by: Carter Cover Designs

Edited by: Alyssa Skaggs

About Melony Ann

Melony Ann began writing short stories and poetry as a child. She continued honing her craft over the years until she took the plunge and began publishing her work, despite having severe anxiety.

Melony writes contemporary romance stories that are full of suspense and a lot of steam.

When she isn't writing, she is loving her family and working to make her life something she deserves.

Melony believes that if her writing can inspire just one person, then all of her hard work is worth it.

Her hope is that her writing allows each and every one of her readers to escape for a little while. To dive into a different world one book at a time.